Gambling on Her Bear

Shifters in Vegas
Book 2

von Anna Lowe

Contents

Other books in this series

Shifters in Vegas

Paranormal romance with a zany twist

Gambling on Trouble

Gambling on Her Dragon

Gambling on Her Bear

Gambling on Her Panther

www.annalowebooks.com

Free Books

Get your free e-books now!

Sign up for my newsletter at *annalowebooks.com* to get three free books!

- *Desert Wolf*: Friend or Foe (Book 1.1 in the Twin Moon Ranch series)

- *Off the Charts* (the prequel to the Serendipity Adventure series)

- *Perfection* (the prequel to the Blue Moon Saloon series)

Chapter One

"Are you crazy?"

Karen winced, remembering her sister screeching the words.

Yes, she was crazy to have come back to Vegas after barely escaping with her life. But three motives kept pulling her back.

A diamond, revenge, and true love. A potent — and possibly lethal — combination.

She eyed the distance from the thirty-six-story rooftop she was perched upon to the twenty-nine-story building across the boulevard. Crap, it was a long way away.

"I can do this," she tried convincing herself.

With a gulp, she glanced down the sheer drop to the street far below. Crowds milled on the sidewalks. The red brake lights of cars backed all the way down the Strip, and the neon lights of casinos blinked, outshining the stars. The whole place was like a carnival plonked down in the middle of the desert, hundreds of miles from anywhere — except the gateway to hell.

Karen inched closer to the edge of the roof. The midnight breeze tugged at her clothes, trying to draw her over the edge and into thin air.

"Not far to glide. Not far at all," she murmured as her knees wobbled away.

Damn it, dragons weren't supposed to be afraid of flying.

What about half dragons? her inner wimp asked.

She brushed back her hair and scowled into the night. Why couldn't she be like her sister, Kaya? Kaya could swoop and soar and climb high into the sky. Kaya wasn't afraid of anything.

Neither am I, her pride shot back. *Not afraid of anything.*

Except maybe her own shortcomings. But hell, it wasn't her fault she was only half dragon. And it wasn't her fault that the other half of her DNA didn't help when it came to aerial pursuits.

She tried visualizing success. That was supposed to help, right? She pictured her leathery dragon wings spread wide and her wide dragon nose pointing the way. Her sleek body would slip gracefully through the air...

But, *boom!* Her visions ended in a hard crash every time. The kind of crash even a shifter couldn't recover from.

With an effort, she dragged her eyes away from the sheer drop. She had to focus on the rooftop across the street: the Scarlet Palace — Vegas' brightest casino on the outside, and the shadiest on the inside.

Focus, damn it. Focus!

The only thing that mattered was the diamond and taking revenge. One quick in-and-out caper and she would leave Sin City forever.

A tic in her right eye reminded her that the first quick in-and-out caper she'd tried pulling off in Vegas had turned into ten days of captivity. She rubbed it away furiously. Revenge was the important thing.

Don't forget my mate! her inner dragon cried.

"Oh, for goodness' sake," she muttered.

You'd have thought being half dragon would mean only a faint inner voice to contend with, but no. The beast thought it was entitled to share every opinion — insistently — even though it couldn't fly properly.

She checked the height and distance again. God, when was the last time she'd attempted anything like this? It felt like years. Wait a minute, it had been years.

"Some dragon you make," she muttered at herself.

The beast glowered inside. *I can breathe fire.*

Well, at least there was that.

You have to believe to be able to fly.

Karen snorted and pushed the beast back into her subconscious. She didn't believe for one second. Sure, she could hold her wings wide and *glide* if the wind was going the right way.

But actually flying — as in, gaining altitude, propelling herself, or accurately controlling where she went? No way. She'd tried a hundred times and had the scars to prove it couldn't be done. Not by a mere half dragon, anyway.

We can do it! her dragon insisted. *Remember that time with Grandpa?*

She snorted. Sure, she'd once climbed a couple of hundred feet and managed a wobbly turn under her grandfather's guidance. But that was only because he'd been there willing her along with his legendary power. She'd been scared stiff the entire time.

Of course, you can't fly if you're scared, her dragon chided. *Remember what Grandpa said?*

Yes, she remembered. *It's just like breathing fire. A dragon's powers are kindled by love, and if you truly believe...*

Sure, believe. The last time she'd believed, she'd been drunk. Drunk enough to try flapping her wings and really flying.

And it worked! her dragon shot back. *You have to trust me. Better yet, get mad at something. Really mad. That works, too.*

She snorted. Her last attempt at real flight was five years ago, and believing had worked for about thirty seconds until she'd panicked in midair. She'd ended up crash-landing in a manure pit and almost breaking a leg.

So, no. She didn't believe she could fly simply by wishing it. And she didn't believe in destined mates, either. That sinfully hot bear shifter she'd hooked up with two weeks ago wasn't her mate. He was just some random guy.

A really, really hot guy, her dragon said. *Remember those hands? Those shoulders? Those checkerboard abs?*

She shook her head. He was just a one-night stand who hadn't even bothered to turn up to a second date, and she was not going to waste any more time thinking about him.

How can you not think about those hazel eyes? her dragon cried. *How can you not think of his touch?*

She bit back a sigh, thinking of the barely leashed power behind his reverent caresses of her skin, her hair. Her whole

ANNA LOWE

body, damn it.

How could you not think about that voice?

His aged-hickory, smoky voice that had whispered in her ear. *This isn't chance. This is destiny.*

He'd said it like he was so sure, and she'd nearly believed. That there was such a thing as love at first sight. That the man she'd surrendered every inch of herself to within two hours of laying eyes on could only be her mate.

Remember the way he looked at us? her dragon went on.

In her dreams, she still saw his dumb struck look, the wonder in his eyes.

Destiny, the wind whistled in her ear.

Her dragon nodded. *Destiny.*

Karen closed her eyes, lost in the memories. Then she snapped them open and swung her arms wildly, finding herself teetering on the edge of the drop.

Crap! She scooped at the air and wrenched her body back just in time to avoid toppling over into thin air.

Focus, damn it! Focus!

If it was destiny, why hadn't he bothered showing up the day after?

She shook her head and looked down. The red-lit fountains of the Scarlet Palace bubbled and danced, taunting her. Traffic proceeded slowly, taking no note of her, and a motorcycle sped down the street.

Diamonds. Revenge. That's what she had to focus on, not this mate nonsense.

She narrowed her eyes on the penthouse apartment of the casino. She'd show those damn vampires what she was made of. Which meant focusing on her plan. A plan which didn't require any flying at all. Just a little gliding. And gliding, she could do. Her grandfather had coached her through it plenty of times. She closed her eyes and remembered his little winks, his bolstering words.

You're a fantastic glider, sweetheart. A real champ.

Well, *champ* might have been overdoing it, but yeah, she could glide.

4

She checked the distance again, licked a finger, and tested the wind. Perfect. She could do it. She *would* do it. Never mind that she'd never tried gliding that far or over quite as high an abyss.

She stripped out of her clothes slowly, bundled them together, and stuck them under one foot. No sense shredding them to bits when she shifted. Plus, she would need them when she reached the roof of the Scarlet Palace.

The night air was cool, and she shivered, standing naked at the edge of the high-rise.

Some dragon you make, a little voice taunted from the back of her mind.

She straightened, took a deep breath, and pulled her inner dragon forth.

Her arms lifted and stretched. Her mouth opened in a silent cry as her body transformed. She wiggled her rear and stretched tall — impossibly tall and impossibly sleek, just like she wished her human body could be. The wind went from ruffling her hair to tickling her long ears and snout, and when she coughed, a tiny spark flew out into the night. The sounds of the city grew louder, the lights brighter, and her skin burned as her leathery hide emerged, armoring her.

She lifted her wings, threw back her head, and bellowed into the night. *I am dragon! Hear me roar!*

For a moment, she allowed herself to revel in the sheer power of being a dragon. No need to worry about attracting attention; the city was far too noisy for that. She could do it! Yes, she could! She would break into the penthouse apartment of the Scarlet Palace and exact her revenge on the vampires. She would escape unnoticed into the night. She would—

Find my mate and take him with me!

Karen scowled at her stubborn dragon. That was the risky part of shifting — the stupid beast was harder to manage when she ceded control of her body. Well, fine. She would deal with that later. Right now, she had other things to think about, like gliding four hundred feet across thin air. Like avoiding more vampires. Like finally exacting her revenge for ten miserable days of captivity. Ten days of pretending she was one-hundred-percent dragon with blood too pure for vampires to drink.

She clutched the bundle of clothes in one claw, shuffled closer to the edge, and started a countdown.

Five. . . four. . .

Man, it was a long way down.

. . . three. . .

God, her sister was right. She really was crazy.

. . . two. . .

She leaned forward and stretched her wings wide.

. . . one!

She gulped and launched herself into thin air.

Chapter Two

For one startling second, Karen thought she would plummet like a stone. A very naked stone that would shatter on the sidewalk and feature in front-page news. She could already see the headlines: *Crazed twenty-nine-year-old dies in attempted "dragon" flight!*

She gritted her teeth, stiffened her wings, and miracle of miracles, caught enough of an updraft from the heated sidewalks below to glide. She wobbled right, dipped left, then banked and steadied out.

I can fly! I can fly! her soul sang in glee. *I can do it!*

The wind tickled the smooth undersides of her wings and cooled her belly.

See? You just have to believe, her dragon said, sounding smug.

She chastised herself for having been too scared to try for so long. Her sister Kaya was right. There was nothing to it. Now that she'd caught the wind, it all seemed so easy. So natural and effortless she was even tempted to flap her wings and try flying for real. Maybe if she practiced more often, she could actually do it. Maybe she wasn't totally useless as a dragon, after all.

You have to believe, her grandfather used to tell her. *Whatever you believe in, you can do.*

A thousand heady images filled her mind as she soared over the blinking lights and fountains that seemed placed there soley to cheer her on. Once she pulled off her plan, she just might head to the Pacific Coast. Better yet, the East Coast — to some long, soft beach not too far from Kitty Hawk, where she would fly and fly and fly. Like the Wright brothers once had,

she would start with low, short flights and work her way up —
literally. Shewould whip herself into flying shape. That's what
she would do. She would learn all the moves her sister made
look so easy and—

The light desert breeze wavered, and she dipped right, losing altitude.

"Shit!"

The roof of the next building was no longer below her, but
above. And crap, she was making a beeline for the windows
of the penthouse. The idea had been to sneak in and out with
her prize, not to shatter hundreds of square feet of glass in the
world's most botched attempt at a burglary. She would have
security on her in no time—

Her skin heated at the double entendre. Security...on
her... If it was a certain ursine member of security, then
having him on her wasn't a bad image at all.

Dammit, Karen! she yelled at herself. *Get your mind out
of the gutter and concentrate on flying!*

Gliding, her dragon sniffed.

Whatever. She strained every muscle as the building
loomed closer. Closer...

Oh God. She was going to crash.

Just concentrate, already!

She squinted at the metal siding of the top edge. Just a
little higher... A little closer...

She could see right into the opulently furnished living room
of the penthouse suite — and shit, if she didn't watch it, she
would crash-land on that huge marble coffee table instead of
the wine-red couch overflowing with pillows of the same rich
color. She would send the crystal vases of flowers flying —
black flowers, because vampires only decorated in black and
red. Knowing her luck, she would end up wedged between the
faux Greek statue standing in a corner and the ceiling-high
speakers taking up most of one wall. Security come
rushing in, followed by the vampires, and she would be taken
captive. Again.

Her lips curled back as she battled for another millimeter
of height.

Whatever you believe in... Her grandfather's voice echoed through her mind.

She hurtled onward, having a really, really hard time believing in anything but what a bad idea this had been. Her sister was right, calling her headstrong, impulsive, and naïve.

Her long dragon ears lay flat along her scalp as she fought for every inch of airspace.

Come on. Come on...

Closer...

She folded her claws flat against her belly, straining for a more streamlined shape, and her angle on the penthouse changed slightly.

She was gaining altitude! She was doing it!

The building loomed closer, just a few yards away now, but crap, it would be tight. Would she splat against the side or careen to safety on the flat rooftop?

Fly! Fly! Fly! she half cheered, half prayed.

Technically, this is only gliding, her dragon commented, completely unimpressed with the severity of the situation.

So glide, damn it! she screamed. *Glide!*

She thrust her nose forward and sucked in her belly. Her hide just about scraped the edge of the building, but she cleared it, and suddenly, the ground wasn't thirty stories down any more. It was just a few inches away.

Too low to the roof to make a proper landing, she tumbled head over heels and crashed to a stop against an air duct.

She lay still, panting wildly, listening for alarms. Looking up at the stars, wondering why she'd ever thought this was a good idea. A good thing none of her relatives had been there to see her land like a clumsy albatross and not a mighty dragon. And damn, did the truth hurt — more than the cuts and scrapes on her body. She couldn't fly. She could barely even glide. What did she think she was doing here?

Um, revenge? her dragon tried.

She sighed and dusted herself off. Right. Revenge.

Lifting her dragon snout, she puffed stubbornly into the night and shifted back into human form. The sharp edges of her claws rounded and became fingers. Her tough hide turned into softer skin, and her hair flowed in the light breeze. The horizon dimmed slightly as her vision switched over, too, and her shoulders throbbed with the exertion of holding out her wings.

She looked back to the rooftop she'd started from, and it seemed a long, long way away. A wave of exhilaration swept through her. She'd done it!

Hurrying with fresh determination, she retrieved the bundle of clothes that had tumbled away in her sloppy landing, yanked them on, and strode toward the service door on the roof, giving herself a pep talk as she went.

Flying in was the hardest part. The rest will be a piece of cake.

The door was locked, of course, but not for long. She grinned, remembering the time her cousin Rudy had taught her that handy lock-opening trick. She pulled the door open and peered down into a dark stairwell, stiffening at the ammonia scent that reached for her from inside. Vampires had no scent, except for that faint ammonia odor that gave them away.

Easy, she lied to herself, advancing slowly.

The night breeze sneered as it slammed the door shut, plunging her into darkness.

"So, so easy," she whispered to herself. She would be in and out in no time. Right?

Chapter Three

Tanner thumped his glass down on the bar and glanced at the ceiling as some vague sensation called to him from above. He tugged at his collar. Damn, it was hot inside the casino. Not to mention noisy, stuffy, and much too bright.

I hate Vegas, his inner bear grumbled.

No kidding. The place just wasn't natural. If it weren't for the motorcycle that allowed him to escape into the surrounding wilds from time to time, he would go nuts. But his clan had sent him down to Vegas for a reason, so he had to to get the job done — then hightail it back home and never leave again. Bear shifters belonged in the woods of the Bitterroot Mountains, not squeezed into suits and ties.

A thin hand slinked over his shoulder and fondled his collar as a sultry voice whispered in his ear. "Hey, Tanner."

He eased away and cleared his throat. "Hi, Amber."

"Hey, baby." The showgirl grinned and leaned in for a kiss.

Tanner turned just in time for her to hit his cheek, not his lips. With one hand, he held her arm, keeping her just far enough away to keep those fake boobs from brushing up against his chest. With the other hand, he pushed away the ostrich feather tickling his head. Amber's headdress was full of them, sticking up like a gaudy crown. All of them XXL, unlike the tiny scraps of fabric barely covering her private parts.

"Hi," he said, keeping his voice flat.

It wasn't that he didn't like Amber. He just didn't like her *that* way. Like a lot of the girls in the Scarlet Palace Revue, she was down on her luck, desperate for any way to get ahead. She had a kid to take care of, too. From what he heard, she

11

sent most of her money to Oklahoma to pay for the child she couldn't take care of herself.

The thought made his heart weep. Kids belonged with their moms. Families belonged together. And fathers sure as hell needed to stick around to care for their own.

He looked around the bar and shook his head. Humans could learn a thing or two from bears.

Of course, not everyone in sight was human. Two of the waitresses — the ones with long legs, short skirts, and bouncing strides — were gazelle shifters, and the balding cashier with beady eyes was a hyena. They remained in human form at work, but he could tell by the scent. The gay bartender sporting a pirate look today was a unicorn shifter, and the big one with curly hair was a bison.

Tanner sighed. He'd seen just about every kind of shifter in the two months he'd been in Vegas. And while every one of them had a story, none of them was his kind. Yes, there were a few bears here and there, but none from Idaho, and none ever stopped to consider how crazy Las Vegas was.

Especially this place. Scarlet Palace. What the hell was he doing, working for a casino run by vampires?

He shook his head at himself, remembering why. He was helping his bear clan, that's what. It had been all planned out — an inside job to get the money they so desperately needed to protect their homelands from vampires — and he'd been the one entrusted to see it through.

Amber sidled closer, and he stiffened — and not in the good way. If only she'd understand that he kept an eye out for her for her own sake, not because he wanted the only reward she had available to give.

"How about you and me—" she cooed in his ear.

How to tell a woman you weren't interested without hurting her? How to tell her you loved somebody else?

"Look, Amber—" He shut his mouth abruptly. Whoa. Had he just told himself he loved someone? He couldn't be in love with the woman he couldn't get out of his mind. Just because he'd had the greatest night of his life two weeks ago. . .

His bear sighed. *One week, five days, and ten hours.*

Tanner shook his head. The bear was mixing up lust with love. He barely even knew the woman.

Love my mate, his bear sighed dreamily. The beast was half hibernating, shutting himself away from the glamour and glitz of Vegas. Unlike that time two weeks ago when the beast had come roaring to the surface, insisting the woman he'd just met was his mate.

It was ridiculous how quickly his bear had been convinced she was the one.

The way she smiles at us. The way her heart speeds up then slows down. The way her eyes shine... She's our mate.

Not our mate, he insisted. *And besides, she would only have jeopardized our plan. It's for the best that she left.*

Even though he was just thinking the words, not saying them, it was hard to keep his inner voice from cracking. The same way it had been damn near impossible to stand her up on their second date. For her own safety, he had to keep away from her.

Safe. His bear nodded. *She's someplace safe now. But when we're done with this job—*

He made a face. Sometimes it felt like he would never finish this job.

—when we're done with this job, we'll find her and make her ours.

If only it were that simple. The job he'd been sent to do involved stealing nearly a million dollars back from the vampires of Scarlet Palace, which would be hard enough. And to find the woman he craved afterward would be like searching for a needle in a haystack. She could be anywhere...

Anyway, that woman was no good for him. The minute he was done with Vegas, he would head home and settle down with a nice she-bear from his clan, not a spitfire who couldn't hold her tongue.

He grinned in spite of himself, just thinking of some of her lines.

You're looking pale, he'd heard her say to a vampire. *Why don't you get some sun?*

13

When he'd asked if the ground was too hard that night they'd spent under the stars, all she'd said was, *I can bearly feel it.* Then she'd grinned, delighted with herself. *Get it?*

Yeah, he got it all right. Everything she said or did went right to his heart.

"Someone's in love." Randy, the gay bartender, chuckled at him.

Tanner scowled and checked his watch. He wasn't in love. He was almost late for his second round of the casino. Time to get moving.

"See you soon, baby?" Amber clutched at his sleeve.

He slipped away, straightening his tie. "Sure."

He could feel Amber watching his ass — Amber or Randy, or worse, both of them. He turned the corner as fast as he could, squinting as he went. The slot machine hall was lit by the brightest, most hysterical lights in the entire casino. The sounds that accompanied them were just as bad: the crank of a slot machine arm, the pings and rattles as the cylinders turned, the firehouse alarms that announced the occasional win.

"Come on. Come on. . . " A balding hedgehog shifter pulled a handle and murmured as apple and orange symbols flashed before his eyes.

"Just one more time," a young man told his girlfriend, feeding yet another quarter into the slot.

Tanner shook his head. When would they learn? Gambling never paid.

"My lucky night," a tattooed man said, grinning at the glassy-eyed raccoon shifter at the machine next to his. The raccoon was in human form, but just barely. The rings around his eyes were dark and heavy, and his nose twitched.

Tanner double-checked the human's face for any sign of shock or recognition of the shifter, but the magic was holding up. The vampires who owned the casino hired a couple of witches to keep their casino laced with just enough magic to keep the human guests blind to any slip in shape from the handful of paranormals in their midst.

Tanner glanced toward the nearest security camera. The feed went right to a control room staffed by two — a vampire security guard and a witch who kept an eye on the cloaking spell. He scowled. The only paranormal being you could trust less than a vampire was a witch, and he hated both.

So what the hell was he doing, working for the bloodsuckers who owned this joint?

Watching. Waiting. The words of the clan elders echoed in his ears. *Planning for exactly the right moment to strike.*

He glanced at his watch again — not the time, but the date. If all went as planned, he would have his chance in forty-eight hours. Everything was arranged, down to the last detail. As long as nothing unexpected arose, he would finally be done with his mission.

The problem was, this was Vegas, where the unexpected was pretty much par for the course.

He threaded his way past the crowds at the slot machines and continued into the roulette hall, staying vigilant. The vampires had hired him as security, and he couldn't let on that he had ulterior motives. Not until the moment came to act on his carefully laid plans.

"*Rien ne va plus.*" A silver ball flashed as the dealer at the nearest table called for last bets.

Half a dozen hopeful faces followed the ball as it rolled around and around. Tanner hid a hopeless shake of the head. Didn't they know the tables were rigged?

The dealer grinned, showing fangs none of the humans noticed. Another vampire. Tanner figured he would never get used to vampires, and he would never, ever consider one harmless. Not even this one — a vampire low on the local totem pole.

He meandered through the hall, checking the guests, the dealers, the wait staff.

"Suspect everyone," the big boss, Igor Schiller, had told him when he'd first been hired.

It had taken all of his self-control not to blurt back something like, *Starting with you.*

Not that he feared the vampires physically. It would take several to overwhelm a bear of his size, for one thing. And secondly, Tanner was off-limits as vampire prey.

"Company policy," Schiller had said. "No feeding off employees."

As if that made him feel better. But he'd nodded and played along, because he had to. To Schiller, he had to be just another big, dumb bear looking for a security job. And it had worked. He'd quickly moved up the ranks to exactly the position he needed to pull off the job he had in mind. The vampires had pulled a sneaky move to steal rights to a swath of pristine wilderness that bordered his clan's property, so it was only fair for Tanner to plot a sneaky move to secure that land once and for all.

Forty-eight hours from now, he would do just that. If things went as planned. If he kept his cool. If the vampires' suspicions weren't aroused.

His bear shook his head. *A hell of a lot of ifs.*

He scratched his ear in hearty agreement. Bears were risk averse, meticulous planners. Hell, you had to be if you wanted to hibernate for six months of the year. Not that Tanner ever did, but it was in his blood.

A bear that plans ahead, gets ahead, his dad used to say.

In fact, just about every bear in the Rockies said that. And if the young up-and-comers ever complained about life being predictable or boring or dull, the elders would shoot them right down.

Predictable means your plans were well laid. Careful means you'll never be burned. Boring means safe.

And they were right, as every bear learned sooner or later. Tanner sure had. He couldn't wait to get home and live the good life again.

"Lucky number sixteen!" A man raised his fist in a cheer as the roulette ball came to rest.

Tanner nodded in greeting to the security guy in the corner and continued to the blackjack hall.

Business as usual? he asked the quick-handed panther shifter dealing cards in the back corner, shooting the question right into his mind.

Dex took care not to look directly at him, answering with a tiny nod. *Another few days of this shit and we're out of here.*

He didn't approach Dex's table because the vampires were vigilant, and if they realized he and the panther were up to something, they would both be shit out of luck.

Another forty-eight hours. He nodded.

The countdown begins, Dex replied as he turned over a card.

"Ace. Twenty-one," Dex announced to the customers at his table.

"Shit!" The man in the middle seat punched the table and threw down his cards.

"Sir," Dex murmured in warning as he swept a pile of chips away.

"What? I'm sick of this shit," the sore loser went on, leaping to his feet.

Two security guards — humans — moved in, flanking the man. Big, linebacker types who stood eye to eye with the equally burly guest.

"Why don't you come with us?" one of the guards said.

The man only grew angrier. "I swear this place is rigged. I'm fucking tired of being cheated!"

Tanner sighed. No, these blackjack tables weren't rigged. They just had extremely crafty dealers, like Dex — the accomplice his entire plan hinged on.

The security guards reached for the man's arms, but he jerked away. He stood tall, practically steaming from the ears, and threw his hands up in a ready-to-attack pose.

"You trying to intimidate me? I know karate! I know jui-jitsu!"

The nearest guests backed away, while others turned in eager anticipation of a fight.

Tanner moved in and fixed the man with a glare.

"I can take you," the human said, then faltered when he saw Tanner looming a few inches above the other two. "I can... Um, I..." he stuttered, waving his hands.

You'll what? Tanner let his eyes say. He squared his shoulders, letting them strain at the fabric of his suit.

The man's eyes widened, and Tanner nearly chuckled. He would love to see the guy react to his bear coming out, but of course, he couldn't do that. And anyway, he didn't need those extra couple of inches. His human form was enough.

The man's shoulders slumped as his eyes hit the floor in submission, a gesture Tanner had seen so often in his time. Even at home with the bears of his clan, it was a regular occurrence. His cousin might be the one poised to take over as alpha someday, but Tanner was the powerhouse everyone counted on to get jobs done.

"I'll just be going now," the sore loser murmured, following the guards' gesture toward the casino doors.

Dex opened a fresh deck of cards and tapped them on the blackjack table. "Next round, ladies and gentlemen. Next round."

And just like that, it was back to business as usual. At least, for about thirty seconds, when the piercing sound of a fire alarm shot through Tanner's earpiece.

He winced and tapped it, moving into a service hall out of sight of the guests.

"Confirm alarm. Confirm," he barked into the tiny mouthpiece.

"Fire alarms registering on the twenty-eighth floor," the guard reported. "Wait — and the twenty-seventh, too."

Tanner glanced up, and for some reason, his heart thumped in recognition. He frowned. What now?

Chapter Four

Feet pounded down the hallway as the casino's crisis crew jumped into action. Calling the police or fire department was always a last resort in a place run by vampires.

"What does Code Blue say?" Tanner demanded.

Code Blue was their code name for Edwina, the aging witch with the dye job gone wrong. She sat in the control room, keeping an eye on the casino along with the guards. Or keeping as much of an eye out as an aging witch could be expected to while clacking away at her knitting.

"She's calling it a Type Four fire. She's trying to fight it now."

His brow furrowed. Type Four meant a fire kindled by supernatural means, not a dropped cigarette or short-circuit kind of fire. And the witch *trying* to fight it most likely meant failing, because good witches were hard to find, a fact his boss constantly bemoaned.

Tanner headed for the stairwell and bounded up the stairs, quickly catching up with the crisis crew. Tenth floor... fifteenth... seventeenth...

"Intruder! Intruder alert!" a new report sounded in his ear.

A fire and an intruder? What was going on?

"Which floor?"

"Twenty-ninth."

The penthouse level? What thief would be crazy enough to sneak into a vampire's private apartment? And not just any vampire, but Igor Schiller, the sneakiest, most bloodthirsty, most malicious vampire of them all. The guy toyed with humans the way a cat played with prey. Even Tanner got the creeps around him. A good thing Schiller was off at a gala dinner. Tanner didn't need to deal with an intruder and Igor Schiller at the same time.

"Crew six to the fire," he told the guard. "Crew four, you head to the penthouse."

"They're already on it," the guard confirmed.

His skin prickled in warning as he neared the penthouse, and he wondered who the intruder was. A rival vampire, maybe? A powerful supernatural of some kind? But truly, what was there to steal in Schiller's apartment other than some really bad art?

He slammed open the fire door at the penthouse level. The moment he stepped into the hall, he heard a woman yell. She was angry, all right. Downright incensed. Furious. Which she had every right to be, if she was Elvira, Schiller's bloodsucking consort who shared the penthouse with his boss.

But it wasn't Elvira. This woman's voice was lower. Stronger. Huskier. This woman's voice reached deep into his soul and warmed every drop of blood instead of turning it to ice.

He stiffened in incredulous recognition. No way. It couldn't be.

"Get your dirty hands off me!" the woman yelled, making the bison shifter guard coming around a corner wince. Tanner stood rooted to the spot, hoping against hope that the person who appeared next wasn't who he thought it must be. She ought to have been miles away from Vegas by now.

"Or should I say, get your dirty hooves off me. Off!" the woman snapped.

Another guard appeared, pulling someone along by the arm.

"I can walk, you know."

The thinner arm the guard was holding wrenched itself free, and the woman stepped into view, holding her head high.

She moved with a regal step, like a queen. Not in the snobby, new-money way Elvira did, but with an understated, old-world kind of class that came naturally. Her auburn hair shone reddish-black, and even the fluorescent lights couldn't flatten that rich color. Her lips were full and wide, her cheeks flushed.

Mate! His inner bear jumped up and down in glee. *Mate!*

Karen. God, it really was her. The woman he'd met two weeks ago—

One week, five days, and eleven hours, his bear corrected absently.

—the woman he'd lost his heart to on their very first night together. Their only night together, because everything afterward had gone wrong. Schiller had sent him to supervise an unscheduled delivery of new chips, and when he returned, he discovered Karen had been taken captive by the vampires. He'd spent a week tearing his hair out trying to figure out some way to free her without sabotaging any hope he had of getting the money his clan needed. But Karen's sister had come along and sprung her first, and he figured that was fate's way of assuring him she wasn't his destined mate.

Now, he wasn't so sure.

"I said, let me go!" Karen jerked away from the guard and turned his way.

God, she was beautiful when she was mad. Almost the same kind of beautiful as when she was aroused. He knew. He'd seen her. Held her. Touched her until she came in a shattering high that had him flying out of control too, making him imagine all kinds of impossible things. Like falling in love with a stranger at first sight. Like knowing his life would never be the same. Like wondering if she wanted him as badly as he wanted her. As in, forever.

The second she saw him, her eyes narrowed, and she stopped dead in her tracks.

"You."

Not a greeting. An accusation that came with a couple of crackling sparks that flickered around her nose and mouth.

Yep, his feisty she-dragon was angry, all right.

He nearly slipped up and said her name. He nearly strode over and punched the guard the hell away from her, too, but he caught himself just in time. He couldn't let on that he knew Karen. Not here, in the den of the enemy. He was her only chance, and if he became a suspect, that chance was gone.

21

Shit. If he became a suspect, his chance at seeing his plan through was fried, too. He would fail his clan for the sake of a stranger.

Not a stranger! his bear bellowed. *My mate!*

He clenched his fists, grappling with the beast for control. He had to act with his brain, not with his heart.

But damn, was his heart ready for a fight.

Her best chance comes from us keeping cool, he told his inner bear. *In fact, her only chance comes from us keeping cool.*

The bear huffed in frustration but slowly backed down.

Tanner tried telegraphing with his eyes and shouting into her mind — *Karen! Please, just play along!* — but all she gave him was that slitty-eyed death stare.

"I can't believe you work for the vampires and their Keystone Cops."

He cut her off quickly, barking at the guard. "Where was she?"

"In the boss' apartment, with this." The boar shifter held up something that reflected blue-black in the light.

His breath caught in his throat, and three words slipped out. "The Blood Diamond."

Igor Schiller had recently acquired the diamond, and Elvira had been parading the thing around all week wedged between her meaty tits. It was still the talk of the town — seventy carats, some said, and worth a fortune. Its mysterious origins only served to heighten the hype — an Indian pasha's diamond, or the dowry of an African princess, others said. The story circulating around the shifter world, though, said its unique coloring came from the blood of a dragon.

He looked from the diamond to Karen, whose eyes shone in exactly the same hue.

"That's mine." Karen grabbed for it, but the guard swung it away.

"It belongs to the big boss, lady," the man said.

"Your boss?" she snickered. "Freddy Fucking Fangs?" Then she shook her head. "That diamond belongs to my family."

Her voice wavered a little, and Tanner's heart pinched. Whatever her connection to the jewel, it was a personal one, because Karen never wavered. Karen was tough and brash and ballsy, and she rarely showed her soft side. Not when anyone was looking, anyway.

His bear swelled with pride, watching her stare down a bison shifter twice her size. None of the women at home had that defiant spark. Was he really going to settle down with someone plain and boring?

No way, his bear declared.

Three more guards rushed up, which meant he had no chance to attempt what instinct demanded — namely, grabbing Karen and the diamond and hightailing it the hell out of the place.

"That diamond belongs to my family." She stomped, nailing the guard's foot.

The guard jumped away with a muffled howl as Karen whipped the diamond out of his hand.

"Mine!" Defiance outshone the desperation in her eyes.

One little dragon shifter up against all those guards, and she was holding her ground.

Of course, she is, Tanner's bear hummed.

She backed up a step, then another, ready to flee. But she backed right into the next guard, who caught her wrists. She wriggled and hissed like a banshee, to little effect.

Without thinking, Tanner shoved the guard away. No one was manhandling Karen that way. He growled and stared the guard down with murderous eyes.

No one touches my mate! his bear roared inside. *No one!*

The guard stumbled backward, holding his hands up.

Tanner gritted his teeth. A good thing those assholes couldn't read his mind, because hell, this was no time to give himself away.

He cleared his throat, wrestling for self-control as Karen stared at him with big, round eyes. Her gaze was softer, as if she felt it, too — that warm-bath feeling that seemed to wash over him whenever he came close to her. A feeling of peace and rightness, just like he got when snoozing in the springtime sun back home, when the world around him was full of warmth, freshness, and promise.

God, she was so close. Her minty breath warmed his neck. Her green eyes locked on his. Her hands felt so small in his and yet they fit together just right. The way she would fit tucked up against his chest.

But a dozen questioning eyes burned into his back, and he had to pull away. Everything hung in the balance. His duty to his clan. Karen's safety. The success of the plan he'd been working on for months.

"The boss will want her untouched," he said, trying to cover up his too-gentle hold on her arms.

And just like that, the brilliant green eyes that had gazed at him with hope and wonder slipped over to fury again.

The guards snickered, and his heart plummeted through his shoes. He'd just implied that he would hand Karen over to Schiller like a prize, and the possibilities made his gut lurch. Like Schiller, sucking Karen's blood. Schiller, touching Karen's body. Schiller—

He dragged his thoughts away from those horrors and locked eyes with Karen, trying to make her understand.

I will never let him harm you. I will never let anything happen to you.

But the eyes that gazed back were stony. Cold. Loathing. And shit, could he really blame her?

It broke his heart, but he had to keep up the charade. He was the security chief here. She was the intruder. He would have to find a way to help her escape later. Maybe on the way to the holding rooms. Maybe later that night. Maybe...

Another guard motioned to Karen. "Hand over the diamond, lady."

"Over my dead body," she hissed just as near-silent footsteps edged up from behind.

The guards around him stiffened, and Tanner didn't have to look to know who it was. Only vampires moved with a powerful silence that knifed away every other sound. Only vampires turned the air in a room cold. And only one vampire had that ice-edged voice that made Tanner's blood shiver in his veins.

Igor Schiller, owner of the Scarlet Palace, stepped up and studied Karen with his cobra eyes.

"That, my dear, can be arranged."

Chapter Five

Karen found herself rooted to the spot for a moment, like everyone else in the room. Then she summoned every ounce of dragon willpower she had and held her chin high. Let Schiller stare. Let Schiller threaten. She wasn't scared of him.

But hell, her unsteady knees sure were.

Igor Schiller stood scowling with his arms crossed over his chest. Apart from his pale, alabaster skin, he looked like an Armani model with his black, slicked-back hair and perfectly tailored suit. His eyes were dark, cold, and piercing.

She forced herself to stare right back. "You're recycling old lines, Igor. Kind of takes the punch out of them, don't you think?"

Everything around her seemed to have been put on pause, with everyone frozen in place. The guards, the whirring noise of the air conditioner, the electric hum behind the walls — all of it died away. Even Tanner — big, burly Tanner, who only ever regarded the world with calm, quiet eyes — seemed stuck between the thump of one heartbeat and the next. It was just her and Schiller, staring each other down.

His gaze burned into her, and she could feel the blood in her veins lurch forward, as if the vampire were summoning it closer. Her body wanted to lean closer, too, in some sick answer to his unspoken command. To step closer, tilt her head to one side, and let him bite. . .

She ground her teeth, turned up the voltage on her killer stare, and watched Schiller's eyes register surprise.

That's right, asshole. You're not the only one with power here, she wanted to say. But for once in her life, she kept her mouth shut. Schiller had all the power, while all she had was determination. An uneven match, but damn it, she would go down fighting.

"And you are as trying as ever, my dear," Schiller sighed in that aristocratic Eastern European accent of his. He tapped his long, perfectly manicured fingernails on the glass surface of the chest-high cocktail table beside him. Slowly, thoughtfully.

"Dragons don't try." She echoed one of her grandfather's favorite lines. "We succeed."

"And this is your definition of success?" Schiller pointed to the posse of security guards cutting off every avenue of escape.

Okay, so her diamond heist hadn't gone exactly to plan. She would figure something out. . . eventually.

"The night is young." She shrugged.

"That it is, my dear." Schiller eyed her neck.

A low, gritty sound came from her left, and though she didn't dare look away from Schiller, she could sense Tanner bristling. Barely holding back an open growl — and barely holding back his inner beast, judging by the feral scent wafting off his wide shoulders.

Tanner. Part of her had melted the second she'd spotted him. And damn it, most of her had melted when he'd touched her, because some kind of crazy heat shield started up whenever he came close, cocooning the two of them from the outside world. His deep brown eyes promised her everything, even if his face gave away nothing. The man was a mystery. An enigma. A riddle she had never been able to puzzle out.

But damn, she sure would like to keep trying.

Her dragon hummed deep inside. *Like for the next century or two.*

Did bears even live that long? She had no idea. It was rather a moot point, given the vampires looming all around them. And anyway, Tanner was a jerk, right? He hadn't shown up to their second date, for starters. And worse, it seemed that Tanner worked for Schiller. What kind of self-respecting shifter did that?

But there was something hidden deep in his eyes that said, *Wait. Please. Wait until I can explain.*

As if she had time to wait. As if she wanted to hear a bear out. If he worked for Schiller, he would have known she had been held captive in the casino for ten miserable days. And had the bear so much as shown his face in that entire time? No. All that tough-on-the-outside, sweet-on-the-inside bear charm had been a show. He didn't love her. He didn't care. She couldn't trust him.

But— her dragon protested.

No buts. She had better things to think about than that stupid bear.

She ripped free of Tanner's grip and turned on every watt of defiance in her bones.

"Igor." She made sure to pronounce his name the way he hated. *Ay-gor,* not the Eastern European version with the emphasis on the end.

She allowed herself one moment to enjoy the flicker of annoyance in the vampire's eyes.

"I see you have returned for another visit," he said in that stiff, Count Dracula accent of his.

She snorted and shook her head. "Just passing through. Transylvania just doesn't do it for me." She waved a hand in the stuffy air.

"Such a pity I cannot let you go without treating you to more of our fine hospitality."

Just what she dreaded most.

"Of course, you can."

"Of course, I cannot."

"You must be so busy," she tried. "Sucking blood, rigging poker tables, filing your nails. I'd hate to take up your valuable time."

"So you'll just take one object and be on your way?" Schiller's eyes flickered to the diamond clutched in her fist.

Well, that had been the idea. And damn it, it had all been going so well. She'd started the fire in the corridor below, then darted upstairs when the guards ran off to investigate. She'd disabled the alarms with an old trick her auntie May had taught her a long time ago. The diamond was right where she figured it would be, on Elvira's antique dressing table, and all she had to do was head to the roof and soar to freedom.

Okay, okay, *glide* to freedom, but that would have worked, too.

She hadn't been counting on the goddamn spider web spell Schiller's third-rate witches cast over the place, and that had been her undoing. She'd tripped one of the invisible threads and set off an alarm. Seconds later, she was surrounded by guards.

Guards — and Tanner. What the hell was up with that bear?

"I'd really hate to hold you up," she said to Schiller, faking nonchalance. A tough act, because half her nerves fluttered with fear, and the other half fluttered with desire — the first, aimed at Schiller, and the second, melting for Tanner.

"My diamond!" a shrill voice sliced through the tension in the narrow space.

Karen rolled her eyes. Tanner winced. Even Schiller flashed a pained look before turning to the woman trotting up on high heels.

"It's my diamond." Karen clutched it away from Elvira.

"No, it's mine." The vampiress curled back thick lips to show her fangs. It was startling, the contrast of that ivory against the black line of her lipstick.

Karen snarled right back. Elvira was a conniving leech of a woman who wasn't good at anything but sucking blood — and possibly Igor's dick. An image Karen really, really didn't need right now.

"You could use a new interior decorator for this place," she sniffed at Elvira. "Black and red is so passé."

"You really could use some manners." Elvira left out the *bitch* at the end, but Karen could see it on her lips.

"And you really need to get your Transylvanian accent down," she shot back. "I can hear Brooklyn come through, loud and clear."

Elvira threw a hand over her mouth, looking horrified, and Karen knew she'd hit the nail on the coffin. Wait, wrong expression. Shit, these vampires were getting her all mixed up.

"Kill her," Elvira screeched at Igor. "Drain her of every last drop of dragon blood."

"Hey!" Karen snapped as a guard pried the diamond out of her hand.

The bison handed the stone to Elvira, who pinned Karen with a haughty gaze as Schiller strung the diamond around the creamy white flesh of her neck.

My diamond, bitch, Elvira's eyes said. She held the diamond up, kissed it, and tucked it between her fleshy breasts.

Disgusting, Karen's inner dragon snarled, letting half an inch of her dragon fangs slide out of her gums. No way was she giving up on the diamond. No way was she letting Elvira have the last word.

"Kill her," Elvira ordered. "Drain her dragon blood."

"Sure." Karen held her wrist under Elvira's nose. "Go for it."

Elvira recoiled, and Karen all but crowed in triumph. Her blood was her ace, and she knew it. Vampire legend held that dragon blood was the richest of all — so rich, it could only be consumed by the most powerful vampires.

"All that mercury, coursing through my veins," she snickered, and all the vampires fell back a step.

Schiller's eyes shone in anger and greed. Oh, he wanted her blood, all right. But even he wasn't powerful enough to dare a sip.

She stared the vampire down for another long minute then pulled her hand back. Maybe it was smarter not to dare a hungry vampire. Especially one who ran a casino and might be able to sense a bluff. So far, nobody had called her on it, but if anyone found out she was only half dragon...

Then the dangerous game she was playing would be up. Permanently.

Chapter Six

"Take her away."

Tanner let out a long, slow breath as Schiller gestured to the guards. Christ, he'd never stopped breathing for that long before. An eternity had stretched from the moment Karen stuck out her wrist in defiance to the moment Igor snapped his fingers, and Tanner had nearly jumped forward and throttled Karen in the intervening time. Was she crazy, provoking a vampire like that?

Crazy. His bear nodded. *In the best possible way.*

Well, he'd been a hair away from shifting into bear form and ripping into the vampire. Damn, that would that have felt good. Even if the others eventually tore him to pieces and sucked out his blood, it would have been worth it to save Karen.

But one impulsive act wouldn't have helped, which was the only reason he'd kept his bear leashed.

Damn. He was crazy, risking his heart to a woman like that. He was bound to sprout gray hair and die young from a heart attack she gave him with one of her escapades.

His bear grinned. *Dying young and happy beats old and bored, you know.*

Tanner pursed his lips. Fate was just messing with him. That's what it was. Karen wasn't his destined mate. She couldn't be.

But his bear sniffed her trail dreamily long after she'd been led out of the room. The only reason the beast allowed her out of sight was the knowledge that her dragon blood kept her safe.

"You." Schiller snapped his fingers.

Tanner held back a growl. Boy, would he like to take on the vampire, face-to-face. But fate was messing with him on that count, too, because he had to be sneaky and bide his time. And frankly, it was unworthy of a bear. But he had his clan's welfare to think about, so he held back his tongue — and his claws.

"I want the whole building searched. Find out how she broke in." Schiller ordered.

Tanner pointed straight up. "Well, she is a dragon."

He hid a smile, imagining Karen swooping down on the roof. God, he would love to see her in dragon form. She would have the same reddish-black coloring as her hair, he'd bet. A flap or two of her wings and she would be airborne. What a sight that would be. And what a feeling it would be for his bear to lope along a mountain ridge as she soared overhead. The moonlight would glint off her wings, and they would meet in some lofty place, shift back to human form, and kiss. Kiss and touch and explore, with the earthy scent of dragon mixing with her human scent.

Imagine not one night, but a lifetime of that, his bear sighed.

"Find out who's responsible and punish them," Schiller snapped.

Ah, law and order in the vampire world. So black and white.

Schiller and his entourage disappeared inside the penthouse suite, and Tanner spent the next hour affirming what he'd already surmised. Karen had broken in through the roof, set a fire a few floors down as a diversion, and then backtracked to steal the diamond. The fire would seal the fire doors leading to Schiller's apartment, too, which bought her time to steal the diamond. If she hadn't tripped the witch's trap, she would have escaped with the diamond.

He walked down the ashy hallway of the twenty-seventh floor, telling himself he had it all figured out. Elementary, right?

Except some things didn't add up. The lock on the roof door had simply been sprung as if she'd had the key. And how had she set the fire? Of course, as a dragon, all she had to do was spit a few flames, but the hallways didn't bear the phosphoric scent that went with dragon's breath. Or so he'd heard, because he'd never met a dragon before. They were few and far between, more legend than real life.

She'll be a legend, all right, his bear hummed dreamily.

They would both be legends — Karen and her sister, Kaya, who'd torched half the underground fighting arena Schiller ran in his spare time. Tanner wished he had been able to witness that, but he'd been working in the casino that night. And he would have loved to see Schiller's face as not one but two dragons slipped out of his grasp.

His brow furrowed with the thought. If he had been there, would he have been able to let Karen go?

And now she was back. While part of him cried to see her taken captive again, another part of his soul sang. He had a second chance!

But really, a second chance at what?

At love. At forever, his bear said.

Tanner took the stairs all the way down to the tenth floor, where Schiller kept his occasional "guests." They came in all shapes, sizes — and flavors, he figured, grimacing. And while some came willingly, others had no choice. Like Karen.

The willing ones weirded him out. There had been a whole group of college-age women through his first month on the job, and they'd heartily participated in the sex-and-blood orgies vampires threw. It turned his stomach, but as long as the women were willing and the vampires didn't kill their prey, well, Tanner figured he would keep his mouth shut. With the witches cleansing the victims' memories of anything but wild sex, the vampires managed to hide their true nature from the outside world. Humans were just as ignorant of the existence of vampires as they were of shifters.

Still, it made his skin crawl, imagining what went on behind closed doors. Seeing the glassy-eyed "guests" leave, assuming their weak legs came from a pint too much to drink instead of a pint too little blood in their veins. And to think Karen was locked up there now...

His eyes skipped ahead to the suite at the end of the hall. He didn't have to ask to know where they were keeping her. He could scent her trail.

The scent of my mate, his bear murmured.

He shook his head. At some point, he and his bear were going to have words and finally get things straight. She wasn't his mate. She couldn't be. He was simply going to free her and see her on her way.

Sure. Right. Uh-huh. His bear nodded, pretending to play along.

He would have rebuked it, too, but voices drifted from the enclosed guard station midway down the hall, and he couldn't help but overhear.

"No way is she all dragon," said one hushed but excited guard. A vampire. You could always tell without looking because their voices were unnaturally smooth.

"You're nuts, man," said the second guard. A wolf shifter — the gritty scratch in his voice was a dead giveaway.

Tanner slowed his step and tilted his head.

The young vampire smacked his lips, an annoying habit that told him it was Antoine, one of Elvira's malicious nephews.

"You know what I think?" Antoine said.

"What do you think?" the wolf replied in a disinterested monotone.

"I think she's half witch."

Tanner's body froze. Witch?

"You're nuts, man," the second guard said.

Tanner sure hoped so. The bears in his clan held a deep grudge against witches ever since the time generations ago when a witch had nearly exposed every shifter in the Rockies to humans. Those shifters had only survived by retreating deep into the mountains, away from prying eyes that the witch had made attuned to the subtle differences between humans and shifters — things like the unique glow in a shifter's gaze, the outdoorsy scent, the telltale twitching of noses and ears. They had barely averted disaster. Older folks in remote mountain communities still told tales of werewolves and werebears, though no one believed them any more. A damned good thing, and a damned close call.

Never trust a witch. He remembered his grandfather's bitter tone.

Never trust a witch, his father would echo.

And Tanner never had. Why would he?

His heart skipped a beat. But Karen? A witch?

"A witch," Antoine declared, sounding so sure. But then, the bastard always sounded sure of himself. "How else did she break into the penthouse? That place is a goddamned Fort Knox."

Tanner's mind spun back over his investigation of the upper floors. It couldn't be. Could it?

"And if she's only half dragon, I bet we can drink her blood," Antoine went on.

"You want to be the one to find out the hard way?" the second guard asked.

Tanner's eyes darted down the length of the hall to Karen's suite. The suite was protected from the inside with a spell, but not from the outside. A guard with the key — like Antoine — could enter any time of day or night.

Tanner leaned forward, clawing at his own palms. The sound of fingers scratching over a tabletop carried to his ears, and he winced. Damn those vampires and their groomed nails.

"Just imagine how good her blood would taste. It would be so thick, so rich. . . "

Tanner braced a hand against the wall. He would not rush over and throttle Antoine. Not yet, he wouldn't.

"I can just taste it. . . "

"You guys are sick, you know that?" the wolf shifter said in disgust. "Forget about it."

Heavy silence indicated that Antoine was doing anything but.

"Listen, I'm going to get myself coffee," the wolf said. "Coffee. That's how you get a pick-me-up. Not blood."

Tanner backed around a corner of the hallway, keeping out of sight until he heard the man's steps recede. The elevator

37

pinged, and the doors slid open then closed. Silence ensued but for the beating of his heart.

He pictured Antoine, scheming away. The young vampire was a greedy little prick. Greedy for blood and for power.

Over the past three months, Tanner had learned a lot about vampires — more than he ever wanted to. Drinking blood gave them power, and the more powerful the donor, the greater the drugging effect of the drink. Strong men and women, humans and shifters... vampires weren't discriminating. They sought the most potent blood, the kind sure to give them their greatest highs and the longest lasting boosts to their power.

And dragon blood was the strongest of all. That's why Schiller coveted Karen's blood. The only reason he hadn't fed from her yet was the fear that her blood was too rich, even for him.

When Tanner sniffed the air, he smelled greed and temptation. Vegas was thick with it, but the scent was especially strong and fresh here. The rancid scent came from the guard room where Antoine schemed away.

Another piece of vampire lore spilled out of the recesses of his mind. Vampires raved about the ultimate drop of blood in a person's body as being the richest, most potent drop. They even had a special name for it — *ultimum gutta sanguinis* — and spoke about it like it was the holiest of all holy things. Most vampires had the sense not to bleed their prey dry, the same way most shifters had the sense not to show their beast sides to humans. But young, reckless vampires... Who knew what they might risk?

Young, reckless, and impatient, like Antoine.

Tanner's heart hammered as he tried to figure out what to do. Whether Antoine decided to go after Karen by himself or to share his hunch, Karen was in danger. He had to get her out of there, fast. Witch or no witch, he wasn't leaving her to these thugs.

But how to do that without blowing his cover?

Easy, his bear huffed. *We claw Antoine to pieces and spring our mate free.*

Right. Like that would work. The entire building was already on high alert.

He peered around the corner and looked at the juncture of two hallways where a pair of security cameras panned back and forth. Like so many others in the building, they were out of sync, creating a blind spot every thirty seconds or so — a glitch Tanner had never reported in case he ever needed to capitalize on that oversight.

Like right about now.

He waited for the cameras to pan away, then rushed to the guard room and peered inside. Antoine stood with his back to the door, tapping his long nails on the vampire-friendly, blacked-out window pane.

An easy target, but Jesus, did he dare? If Tanner went through with his hastily formed plan — never a good idea — there would be no turning back. Maybe he should think things through a little.

What, now? his bear bellowed. *This is our chance!*

A chance to screw up everything. Karen could be a witch — a witch who had lied to him. Maybe even a witch who had enchanted him. Was she worth risking the future of his clan for?

Hell, yes! his bear hollered.

Instinct took over, and he rushed in before the vampire could react. The moment Tanner slammed his fist into the back of Antoine's head, the vampire fell with a grunt. It took all his self-control not to keep punching to make sure Antoine would never wake to think bloody thoughts about Karen or any other woman again.

But there wasn't time for that, and killing Antoine would only raise suspicions. Tanner grabbed the master key card, ran to the door, and sprinted down the hallway as soon as the cameras panned away.

"Come on... come on..." He tried the key card in a dozen different positions. The lock light remained steadfastly red. He was running out of time. The cameras were slowly panning his way.

"Come on..." He fumbled one more time.

39

He was about to shoulder the door open when the light flashed green, and a click sounded. He dashed inside, whirling to close the door before the camera caught any hint of activity.

Whew.

Then, *whoa!* Something rocketed from across the room, and he ducked just in time to avoid a vase that shattered an inch over his head. Water splashed his hair, and a tulip whacked him in the ear.

"Bloodsucking bastard—" Karen's shout broke off when their eyes met.

Well, he hadn't been expecting a kiss, but a vase?

He wiped the water off his face and held his hands up, because his green-eyed spitfire had a two-inch-thick glass ashtray in her hand, ready to hurl.

"It's me," he said.

Her eyes narrowed on him, taking aim for her next volley, perhaps.

"You," she uttered, totally unimpressed.

Chapter Seven

Tanner's bear groaned. *She hates us, and it's all your fault!*

"Hey!" he protested.

It wasn't his fault this headstrong she-dragon had been taken captive by vampires — twice. It wasn't his fault he'd had to pretend to play along with the vampires.

"Hey, what?" Karen demanded.

"I wasn't talking to you," he muttered, cursing his bear.

Karen lifted the ashtray and wound up her throwing arm for what was sure to be a hundred-mile-an-hour fastball hurled his way.

"Wait!" He stuck up his hands.

Karen didn't wait, but she didn't throw, either. She stomped right up to him and shoved him back against the door. *Shoved* him, like he was the lightweight and she was the grizzly.

"Now you listen to me, bear," she started.

He could have reacted in any of a dozen ways. He could have pinned her against the door and demanded to know if she was really a witch. He could have grabbed her by the arm, clamped a hand over her mouth, and carried her the hell out of that place. He could have tried to find the words to explain everything that had happened after the night they'd first met. But what did he do?

It happened before he even realized what he was up to. Some hidden switch inside him flipped, and all of a sudden, he was on fire. All the weeks of worrying and waiting, of hoping, fearing, and scheming away. All the hours dreaming of the night he'd shared with her...

All that boiled up out of nowhere, making him crush her close and deliver the mother of all bear kisses. A deep, hungry, possessive kiss that screamed *I'm sorry* and *I love you* and *Please, never throw a vase at me again.*

He begged her. He consumed her. He marked her as his.

A second after Karen squeaked in surprise, her hands fisted in his shirt, pulling him closer. Her mouth opened under his, inviting him to taste her. Demanding that he do so, in fact, and swiping his tongue with hers at the same time. She yanked him closer until her breasts were mashed against his chest, her heart pounding against his, her scent intoxicating him.

He got so lost in that kiss, they just about tipped over, but they both came up for air at the very same time. He blinked at her, and she blinked at him.

"Karen," he whispered.

She opened her mouth but didn't utter a peep. His indomitable she-dragon was tongue-tied, possibly for the first time in her life.

Then the need surged back, and he kissed her again. This time, he held her gently against the door... Or maybe not so gently. He couldn't tell any more, but since the sounds Karen made were of the *More, baby, more,* variety, he kept at it, feeling like he would never get enough of his mate.

His mate. Whoa. Could his mate really be half witch?

Witch. Dragon. Whatever, his bear muttered inside.

All that mattered was that she was his, and he was hers, and that they stayed that way forever.

Forever, his bear murmured, savoring every nuanced flavor in that desperate kiss.

Somewhere in the back of his mind, a gong tolled, informing him that *forever* would end a hell of a lot sooner than he wanted it to if he didn't get his mate out of the Scarlet Palace soon. So he pulled away — really pulled with every muscle in his body, because the magnetic force squeezing his body against hers was that strong. Their lips smacked as they unlocked, and he rested his head against the door, panting against her shoulder.

Must... regain... control... His brain sent the order, but most of his nerves were on strike, refusing to deliver the message. *Mate's... life... depends... on... it...*

It didn't help that her hands still clutched him or that her lips moved softly over his ear the way they did in his dreams.

"Tanner," she murmured, making his soul sing.

No time to sing. Get her out. Make mate safe.

Funny that the bear was the reasonable one for a change.

It took another minute of smoothing a hand over the silky wave of her hair before he really pulled himself together.

"I have to get you out of here."

"We have to get both of us out of here," she replied, and it was so, so tempting. But it couldn't work that way, because he had to stay on the inside and finish what he came to Vegas to do. And how would he ever explain that?

I love you. I want you.

I need you, his bear added.

But I have to let you go. Again.

He didn't bother trying to get any of that out, though. Not now. It was time for action, not words. Nudging Karen behind him, he opened the door and peeked out. He timed the cameras carefully, then hurried her down the hall. A glance into the guard booth showed Antoine still out for the count.

The elevator doors pinged, and he yanked Karen around a corner to the stairs. Any minute now, the second guard would saunter back to his post and raise the alarm. Tanner flew down the stairs four at a time, and Karen kept pace, thank goodness. Hell, being a dragon, she probably could take ten at a time.

Half dragon? Half witch?

No time for twenty questions, though, so he pounded on and reached the ground floor just as his earpiece screeched.

"Alert! Alert! Guard down! Guard down!"

He sprinted down a hallway toward the back, praying they wouldn't be seen. It was about five in the morning, and though the casino never really slept, things did slow down a little around dawn, when most of the vampires would return to their quarters. He took a circuitous route, knowing which hallways had cameras and which didn't.

43

"Tenth floor! Tenth floor!" Another alert came through. "Guard down!"

No one had reported Karen missing yet, but they would put two and two together any minute now.

"Hurry!" he grunted. "Here."

He threw a door open and gulped fresh air, staring at the pale pink glow in the sky. It was amazing how even the streets of Vegas could feel clean and fresh after hours spent cooped up inside. If he ever made it out of this crooked town, he would head back to his mountains and never, ever leave again.

He gulped the sight of Karen, too. Wild green eyes, glossy, auburn hair, freckled nose... Could he really let her go?

Forget about the clan. We'll figure out some other way of getting the money we need. Let's just leave with her, his bear begged.

And dang, he'd never been so tempted to forsake his family as just then.

"Go," he said hoarsely before his heart got the better of him.

"Guest One missing!" A voice boomed through his earpiece. "Repeat, Guest One missing!"

"Go." He motioned toward the sidewalk, where a group of tourists was walking by. Karen could mix with them and flee.

"Wait. What?" She grabbed his arm.

"I have to go back..." he started then stalled out. How could he possibly explain?

"Don't. They'll know you helped me. Don't."

The magnetic force felt stronger than ever. He could feel it in his bones, in his veins.

"I have it all figured out," he lied.

She snorted. "Sure. What are you going to do?"

Yeah, what are we going to do without her? his bear demanded.

"Security team to stations!" The next announcement pierced his ear.

Shit. He had no time. It was now or never.

"You have to go." He meant to say it forcefully, but it came out weak and warbly, not at all fitting for a bear. He settled for pushing her toward the sidewalk instead. Maybe that would work.

She took two steps, then stopped and glared at him. Dammit, his last sight of his mate, and she was glaring at him.

But then her eyes softened, and he swore he could hear her dragon pleading with her the way his bear did with him. *Don't let him go...*

Half dragon... half witch, a little voice reminded him. How could a bear and a witch ever make things work?

Somehow, we'll make it work, his bear shot back. *We will.*

Karen closed her eyes, then nodded silently to herself. Was she thinking the same thing?

When she opened her eyes again, her gaze was firm. Uncompromising. "Meet me tonight. At eight," she said, like she had an internal clock or appointment book or something. "Can you get away by then?"

Another point of no return. He had given her freedom. Now he needed to get back on track.

A bear that plans ahead, gets ahead. The old saying whispered through his mind. And damn it, his plans didn't involve evening meetings with dragons, witches, or anyone else.

Careful means you'll never be burned. He could practically hear the bear elders chanting in his ear. Careful meant letting Karen go.

He opened his mouth, but the word refused to come out. Flat-out refused, like a stubborn dog digging its heels in, shoving its ass down, and fighting against its leash.

So he nodded. "Okay." What else could he do? Hell, yeah, he would get away if it meant seeing her one more time. "Where?"

She snorted. "Some place bloodsuckers would never go."

He wanted to suggest Alaska, but he doubted she would make it that far in the next fifteen hours.

"The Golden Panda," she said before he could come up with anything. A damn good thing her mind was clear enough to decide, because his was still bouncing all over the place. "Off Fremont Street. Ask if they serve dragon soup."

He gaped at her. "Dragon what?"

Now she was the one hurrying away, and he was the one rooted to the spot while her voice carried back to him. "Dragon soup. Golden Panda. Eight o'clock tonight."

She mixed with the crowd, and then she was gone.

∞∞∞∞

Tanner stood still for another long minute — a minute he didn't have — fighting the urge to run after Karen instead of heading back into the casino. Eventually, he managed it, wiping his mouth from the kiss and sprinting back up the stairs. A damn good thing vampires didn't have a keen sense of smell — not for anything except blood — so chances were good they wouldn't scent her on him.

But he sure could. It was heaven and torture at the same time. And man, what a mess. Why hadn't she listened to him the first time around? He'd warned her away from the Scarlet Palace from the start. Why did Karen have to be so infuriatingly stubborn? So reckless? So…so…

Mine, his bear rumbled inside.

He ran up the stairs — a good excuse for appearing breathlessly on the tenth floor — and started berating the men for letting down their guard.

"You what? She what?" he bellowed, making damn sure every accusation was aimed at the two guards.

"I swear, I found him like this…" The wolf shifter motioned toward Antoine, who was propped up against the wall, groaning.

Antoine touched the back of his head gingerly. "She's a witch. I swear she's a witch. How else could she sneak up behind me?"

Tanner held back a snort and let out his best growl as he gestured at the wolf's coffee cup. "You left your post?"

The guard trembled, and the five others who'd gathered around tut-tutted as if they would *never* consider doing such a thing.

"We're reviewing the camera footage now." The voice of the head of security came from a speaker, and everyone hushed.

Tanner, too.

"I'm sending it up to your monitor. Stand by."

The picture on the monitor blinked then showed an empty hallway with a timer on the upper right. It scrolled back in time, then forward from the point that the wolf guard lumbered into view and pressed the elevator button.

"Fuck, man, are you in trouble," one of the guards said, making the wolf groan.

Tanner stood very, very still, staring at the screen long after it showed the guard disappearing into the elevator. His nails bit into his palms, and a fresh line of sweat broke out on his brow. He would be the one in a hell of a lot of trouble if his timing had been off.

"Nothing," one of the men muttered. "Not a damn thing."

He exhaled slowly.

"I'm telling you, she's a witch!" Antoine insisted. "She must have levitated a chair and popped me over the head."

It took everything Tanner had not to smirk. That had been his fist, not a chair. But hell, if Antoine wanted to believe that, it sure suited him.

"How else could she break into the penthouse?" Antoine went on.

That part, Tanner had to agree with, and it made his skin itch. Could it really be?

"I'm telling you, she's a witch," Antoine insisted.

Tanner glared at him, but inside, his mind spun. Shit. Could his mate really be half witch?

Chapter Eight

Karen followed a stumbling group of all-night revelers for five city blocks, then darted down a side street and looked back.

No alarms. No security guards chasing her down. No undercover vampires showing their teeth.

Well, not yet, it seemed.

The only faces she spotted were bleary-eyed and weary — the faces of gamblers and drinkers. Humans, one and all. Some were just waking up, while others were weaving their way home after too many drinks downed and too many dollars lost.

She shook her head, as much at herself as at them. What was she doing in this crazy place?

The sky formed a pinkish yellow backdrop to the blinking lights that never seemed to go out in Vegas. Screaming reds, neon greens, and clamoring blues — a color for every one of her faults, it seemed. God, she had gone and done it again — lost her head to the alluring glitter of it all, but how could she help it? After all, she was half dragon.

And yes, half witch. A second-rate witch whose powers were about as useful as her dragon powers were.

In other words, just enough to land her into trouble, but not enough to get her out.

She took a long breath of air that wasn't as painfully dry as it would be in another hour or two and hung her head. Everything had gone smoothly — well, relatively smoothly — until she'd fucked up. She'd hexed the rooftop lock open — child's play, really — then snuck down the stairwell and set a fire on the two floors below the penthouse. Fire was about the only spell she was good at. Her dragon could cough up enough sparks for her magic to accelerate into a huge, hungry blaze.

49

That was always satisfying — especially this time, because she got to watch Igor Schiller's collection of blood-themed artwork go up in flames.

Then she'd backtracked to the penthouse, managed not to gag at the scent of old blood that permeated the place, and snatched the diamond. Her diamond, damn it. But then she'd tripped the web spell and fucked it all up. That was the problem with being half witch — she could only sense some forms of magic. Others, she was as blind to as a bat.

So she'd lost her chance. No diamond, no revenge.

"Great job, Karen," she muttered. "Great fucking job."

How was it that her brilliant plans didn't quite work out?

At least a guardian angel had been looking out for her. Or rather, a guardian bear.

Right on cue, her pulse skipped and her ears filled with a joyous ring. It was pathetic, really — and confusing as hell — because she'd grown up thinking destined mates were a myth. But then her sister Kaya had gone all dreamy-eyed for a wolf and rode off into the sunset with a blissful look on her face. Not just a *this-guy-knows-his-way-around-a-woman's-body* kind of bliss, but a deeper, soul-soothing kind. The kind that said *forever.*

But, damn. Could it really be that fate had its eye on her, too? It had taken all she had to peel herself away from Tanner after their first night together, and this time had been even harder. She was still reeling from his kiss. Still savoring the faint scent of him on her clothes... and dammit, still dreaming about the way his fingers had traced the contours of her face.

Mate, her dragon purred.

She could just hear her great-aunt Gretchen cackle now. *As a witch, you'll be immune to that fated-mate nonsense so many shifters make asses of themselves with.*

Maybe. Maybe not.

A taxi cruised past, and part of her jumped up and down. *Hail it! Get the hell out of town!*

But she didn't budge, because another voice in the back of her mind chanted Tanner's name over and over. It was just like when she'd tried leaving Vegas with Kaya and Trey a few days ago. That feeling of a rubber band pulling her back to Tanner, refusing to let him go. That *how am I going to survive the next few hours without him* feeling she swore she would never, ever give in to.

And yet, there she stood, pining for her bear in a thousand different ways.

Shit. *Her* bear?

He's ours. And he saved us. Our hero! her dragon crowed.

She snorted. A dragon really ought to have more pride.

He put himself in danger for us!

That part was painfully true. The question was, what was she going to do about it?

She stalked the streets, zigging, zagging, and checking behind her every few seconds. Gradually, she moved away from the high-rise glitz of the Strip and into the seedier side streets of old Vegas.

A ghost dressed in a pinstriped suit and leather shoes meandered past, tipping his bowler hat to her. A rat skittered into the shadows, and a crow cawed overhead. The faint scent of the desert wafted in on the fading morning breeze. Karen tilted her chin up, watching the colors of sunrise blend into the full light of day. A good time to be out — when vampires were not. Still, their henchmen might be out and about, so she didn't let down her guard.

She hustled into a fire red English phone booth on the corner of Eighth and Fremont — the kind with dozens of square windows and a gold crown on the top. A goddamn crown, as if the Queen might turn up in Vegas and make a quick call to Buckingham Palace to check on her corgis.

Karen darted inside and tapped her fingers beside the keypad for a good three minutes. She'd lost her phone sometime in the past few hours. Should she call her sister? Shouldn't she?

Finally, she punched the number. Kaya was an early riser, and she might worry — or worse, grow suspicious — if Karen didn't check in. The last thing Karen needed was her older sister coming to her rescue again. She had gotten herself into this mess. She could get herself out. Right?

She pursed her lips.

The phone buzzed twice before the line clicked and her sister's breathless voice came on. "Karen? Are you okay?"

She rolled her eyes. "Yes, Mom."

"Where are you?"

"Um...Palm Springs. It's great." Karen closed her eyes to the storefronts and the stretch limo rolling through the intersection, imagining golf courses, fountains, and whispering palms instead. So she was fibbing. So what? It was for her sister's own peace of mind.

"So you're out of Vegas? Thank God."

Well, she was out of the Scarlet Palace. Close enough?

"Where are you?" Karen asked, trying to distract her sister.

"Home," Kaya gushed in a way she rarely did. She was the no-nonsense sister, not the impulsive, emotional one. And damn, if Kaya had fallen head over heels in love with a wolf she claimed was her destined mate, what chance did Karen have?

"You should see how clear the mountains are this morning," Kaya said. "The air is so fresh, and the creek is sparkling in the sun..."

Karen pictured the jagged peaks, the babbling brook. She inhaled, imagining the clean mountain air, remembering the timeless peace of her great-great-uncle's old place, which was Kaya's now. Karen had never been interested in ranching, but she'd been ankle-deep in the creek's cool water prospecting for precious gems more times than she could count.

She wiggled her toes in her sandals. Yeah, it would be good to head home. She'd been away too long, chasing rainbows. Looking for something more exciting, though all she'd discovered was that the grass wasn't greener — not in New York, not in Miami, not in LA. And definitely not in Vegas.

"I don't know why anyone would want to live anywhere else," Kaya enthused.

Karen pictured the faraway look on Tanner's face when he'd told her about his mountain home the first night they'd met. He'd gone on and on about the night sky, talking about stars like so many neighbors and gushing about old stands of pine and spruce like they were buddies of his. Her soul hummed just thinking about it. Maybe she and Tanner could head to the Rockies together. She could go back to prospecting. Her dragon had a nose for the best stones and gems, and she'd always earned enough to get by.

Honest work, her dragon nodded.

Right, she snorted. *As if it wasn't your idea to go after the diamond in the first place.*

The diamond is different. It should be in the hands of dragons, not vampires.

And just like that, all her rage and bitterness came back. She would show Schiller and his bloodsucking band what an angry dragon could do.

"How's Trey?" she asked, trying to keep her sister distracted.

A dreamy sigh floated over the line. A month ago, Karen would have rolled her eyes, but now... She remembered the electric hum that warmed her body when Tanner touched her and nearly made the same sound.

Mate, her dragon murmured. *My mate.*

She thumped her head against the side of the phone booth. God, why was the attraction so hard to fight?

Why bother resisting? her dragon shot back.

Because she had her pride. Because Tanner worked for the enemy. Because she had a diamond to steal. Because... because...

No matter how many good reasons she came up with, they all fell flat in her mind.

"So you two are off to a good start?" she asked, only half paying attention to the conversation.

"Well, getting this place up and running will be a lot of work," Kaya said. "But it's going great. Really great — having a project to work on together, making a future..."

Karen suppressed a little sigh. Jeez, that sounded nice. She'd spent the last two years bouncing from city to city, looking for something she had never really managed to define.

We were looking for our mate, her dragon whispered.

53

It hadn't felt like that at the time, but the moment Tanner had bumped into her in a Vegas bar, the world had zoomed away, and suddenly it seemed as if every step in her life had been leading toward that momentous occasion. As if fate had been steering her all along. Working the wanderlust out of her system, learning from a thousand bitter mistakes... All so she would be ready to settle down when the time came. With Tanner, her destined mate.

She could picture it perfectly. Him and her, working side by side in a quiet valley at the foot of the mountains. She could prospect for gemstones, and he could log the choicest lumber. They could fix up a little cabin with a big fireplace and huge views and...

Someone tapped on the glass of the phone booth, and she snapped her head up.

"Come on, lady. Finish up." A man pointed to his watch and held an imaginary phone to his ear, then showed her his cell phone. "My battery is dead."

He was just a harmless human, but Karen's gaze quickly swept the street. She'd better get out of sight and on to Plan B — or Plan L or Q or whatever letter she was up to by now. It seemed like she'd spun through the entire alphabet once already and was starting all over again.

"Listen, Kaya, I'd better go. Say hi to Trey and take care."

"I will. And you, too," Kaya said. "Stay out of trouble, you hear?"

Karen held back a snort. She was neck-deep in trouble. Again.

She hung up, hurried out of the phone booth, and headed down a side alley for the one place in Vegas she figured she would be safe from vampires.

Hopefully.

Possibly.

Maybe.

She threw a last glance over her shoulder and heard her sister's words echo through her mind. *Stay out of trouble, you hear?*

Chapter Nine

Tanner checked the reflection in a shop window for anyone tailing him as he walked down Fremont Street, trying to amble like a tourist instead of rushing. Which took just about everything he had because his bear was kicking, screaming, and hurrying him along.

Come on, already! Must see my mate!

Dang. How could the beast be so sure? And how could his mate be a witch?

Only half witch, the bear shot back. *Half dragon, too.*

He snorted. As if that added up to a good match for a bear.

She's perfect! the bear said brightly.

She's trouble.

The bear just shrugged, like that didn't matter at all. *She's in trouble. We'll get her out.*

Again, how could he be so sure? And what would his clan have to say about that? He was in Vegas to help his family, not to rescue crazy she-dragon witches.

My she-dragon witch, his bear corrected him.

A car horn tooted, and he jerked his head around. Shit, he really needed to pay attention and make sure he wasn't being followed. Igor Schiller had been furious to find out Karen had escaped, and though all his wrath had been directed at Antoine, you never knew.

Tanner mingled with a crowd then darted down a side street and stood breathlessly in the shadows, checking for any sign of a trace. He'd been careful to park his motorcycle a few blocks away and meander for ten minutes, making sure he hadn't been followed.

No one is following us, his bear insisted. *Let's go already.*

With one last look back, he headed into an alley and took a right turn. And there, marked by red flags, gold statues, and upward sweeping Chinese towers on the false front, stood his destination: the Golden Panda.

The sweet-and-sour odor of Chinese cooking wafted down the alley, which made it the last place a vampire would wander into — no juicy steaks, no sizzling grills. Rice, chicken, and soy sauce were not exactly vampire fare. Karen was a goddamned genius.

Of course, she is. His bear grinned.

He licked his lips. It had been a hell of a long day — plus the preceding night when he'd been on duty — and he'd only managed a quick stop at his room in a seedy boarding house before racing out here. A little chop suey sure would hit the spot now.

When he reached the golden statues flanking the door, though, he paused at the scent of shifter. What kind of shifter, he couldn't tell. Tigers, maybe, like the ones painted on the windows? Dragons? Did Karen have distant relatives here?

He swung the door open, tensing. What would he do when he saw her? What would he say? And what exactly would he encounter inside?

He ducked past a red velvet curtain and looked around. Six plain tables stood on the left and another six on the right, with a total of five guests at them — three on one side murmuring over a mah-jongg board and two on the other, eating expertly with chopsticks. Giant vases filled with bamboo stalks stood in the corners of the restaurant, and the walls were hung with stylized landscapes marked with bold calligraphy. Straight ahead was a counter plastered with photographs that illustrated the meals. In short, it was like any other inexpensive Chinese restaurant in any other place.

Except for the giant panda shifter sitting at the register, chewing a stalk of bamboo. By the time Tanner blinked a few times, though, an elderly Asian man with a long, skinny beard sat where the panda had been, holding a slender pipe in place of the bamboo.

Whoa. Had he been imagining things, or had the guy shifted that fast?

The bead curtain separating the order counter from the kitchen parted, and a young woman wearing a Hello Kitty apron stepped out.

"Welcome to the Golden Panda. A drink for the gentle-bear?"

Tanner tilted his head. Did pandas have as keen a sense of smell as bears, or could she tell what he was through some other means? He ran a quick hand over his chin. There'd been no time to shave before coming out here, but the scruff he felt was man-scruff, not grizzly hair. Huh. Was it that obvious he was a shifter?

He sniffed the air. The three guests huddled on the right had to be pandas, too. The two on the left with funny mustaches were... primates of some kind. Which stumped him. What kind of primates had hair that spiked straight up from their heads and mustaches that flared out at the sides?

"Um..." He scratched his head, trying to get back on course. "I'd like some dragon soup."

He felt silly uttering the words like some kind of spy code, but if it meant seeing Karen again...

The woman's eyes narrowed. She gave him a slow once-over then exchanged a few words with the old man in Chinese.

"Just a moment, please," she said, heading toward the kitchen again.

The beaded curtain closed behind her, and through it, Tanner swore he saw her body change into a furry, black-and-white form. A panda in a Hello Kitty apron?

He stepped aside to wait, studying the photographs on one wall. At first, he figured they were nature shots of pandas in the wild, but soon he came to suspect they were vacation shots of some kind. He could just imagine the narrative that might accompany them. *There's Grandpa with the nephews in Sichuan Province...*

Below the panda photos was a framed poster that had to have come out of a National Geographic magazine. *Mammals of Greater China,* it read, with pandas, tigers, and... Tanner leaned in to find out what those mustached monkeys were. *The Francois Langur, or Leaf Monkey, is the least studied of subfamily Colobinae...*

He shot a glance over to the two men sipping green tea, then back at the poster. Leaf monkeys, huh?

His bear shrugged. *As long as they're not armed with throwing stars, no problem.*

"This way." The woman in the apron returned and pointed him down a side hall.

His heart beat faster as he walked through the narrow space. It smelled of incense, ginger, and jasmine tea. All so unfamiliar, so hard to read.

"Hello?" he called, reaching a round room set up for private parties with rich, luxurious decor. The only thing that didn't fit amidst the plush couches around the sides and the bouquet of exotic flowers on the center table was the cheap playpen. Two fluffy panda babies peered out at him with big, round eyes.

The one on the right yawned and blinked its black-ringed eyes, while the other waggled its oversized ears and squeaked.

"Um, hi," Tanner murmured, looking around.

A dozen rooms with frosted glass panes set in the doors branched out from that central space, and all were closed except one. He stepped over, and his breath caught in his throat.

The room was wallpapered in rich red and gold and lit with tasseled red lamps. Some had dragons printed on them, others tigers, and they all seemed to aim silent roars at him. But his gaze bounced right past them to Karen, standing at the far side of the small room.

Karen, dressed in a form-fitting red silk dress with a long row of knot buttons fitted into loops, marking little crosses along her body. Karen, looking at him with wide, dancing eyes that might have been as big as his felt just then. Her hair was done up in a bun, and her arms were crossed, as if she was as unsure where to begin as he was.

"Karen," he murmured.

"Tanner," she whispered back.

Just hearing his name on her tongue made the best kind of shiver run down his back. He stepped forward, brushing a lantern with his head.

Karen, he almost said again because suddenly, his mind was blank. Blissfully, innocently blank, like it had been the first time he'd ever laid eyes on her.

Mate, his bear breathed. *Mate.*

Her lips moved, but no sound came out, and all he could think of was her kiss. The testing little kiss she'd given him the first time they'd met and the heated ones that grew out of that in the blink of an eye. He thought of the hungry kisses of their first night and the desperately confused kiss from a few hours ago. All of them blended together and came roaring at him like a blaze, and just like that, his body was on fire again.

Without realizing it, he erased the distance between them and reached for her, and the look on her face said she would respond with a kiss instead of the slap he'd originally feared. But just as his lips brushed over hers — just as their bodies started to mesh — a bang sounded behind him. He whirled, protecting Karen with his body.

A toothless old lady cackled and started lighting the candles set around the room. Candles, like the room needed any more atmosphere or any more heat.

"Eat, eat," the old lady croaked, beckoning them toward the table.

Oh, he'd like to eat, all right. But dumplings and chow mein were not exactly what he had in mind.

"You must be starving," Karen murmured, and his head whipped around. Was she serious or teasing? With her, he never could tell.

Her eyes sparkled and danced, but her body was stiff and erect. About as erect as part of him was just from coming so close to her seconds ago.

Damn. Maybe she was a witch. Maybe she was hexing him.

And then it hit him. *Grandma Mae said love is magic, didn't she?*

There was good magic and bad magic in the world, just like there were good bears and bad. Maybe he ought to give Karen a chance.

You definitely need to give her a chance, his bear said. *Give us a chance.*

He took a deep breath, pulled out a chair for Karen, and hid as much of his faded jeans behind it as he could. There she was, done up like a million bucks, while he looked like some guy off the street.

Her eyes roved over him briefly, and the funny thing was, he could have sworn she didn't mind one bit.

When she stepped past him to take her seat, her scent brushed his body like a blanket begging him to huddle closer and warm up. It took everything he had to push her chair in instead of tilting it backward and kissing her skin. He circled to the chair across from hers at the tiny table, parking a thousand fantasies in the back of his mind for later — vehemently hoping there would be a later. Fantasies of kissing, sucking, and licking the creamy skin just under her ear. Of undoing the bun, threading his fingers through her hair, and pulling her closer. Of touching, sniffing...

He clenched his hands into fists as the old woman banged a tray on the table and poured him a cup of green tea.

"So what will it be?" Karen asked him.

Her nostrils flared, and he wondered if she meant food or something else. And damn did his bear vote for the latter. But he hadn't come to get carried away all over again. He'd come to...to...um...

"You choose," he managed in a husky voice.

When Karen licked her lips and looked at him, he almost lost control. One little swipe of the hand and he could knock the table out of the way and pull Karen into his lap, ready to consume.

She caught her lower lip with her teeth and took a deep breath.

"Ma Po Tofu," she said to the waitress, looking for his okay. "And an order of Beef Broccoli with white rice."

He gave a tiny nod and told himself she was right. They needed to talk. They needed to figure things out. First things first, right?

And second things. . . his bear growled inside, picturing a different kind of feast.

The waitress placed a cup of soup in front of him and left the room. He looked at Karen through the curling threads of steam that rose, separated, and met again. What to say? Where to start?

Karen, are you a witch? One of the thousand questions in his mind muscled its way to the front, but he didn't say it. He wasn't really ready for that one yet.

Karen, do you feel this, too? This unquenchable thirst?

Should he admit it? Shouldn't he?

Karen, are you my destined mate?

If she wasn't, he was going crazy, because no woman had ever done this to him before.

"So," he started slowly, finally pushing a few words through tight lips. "Tell me about that diamond."

Chapter Ten

Karen hid her trembling fingers in her lap and did her best to meet Tanner's level gaze. What she really wanted to do was reach out and stroke his skin. A little swipe of the coarse stubble dotting his chin, a tiny brush of a finger over those perfect, slanting eyebrows. Just a little contact to settle her jumpy nerves.

But touching him would only fan the fire blazing inside her, and she knew it. He was so temptingly close, and as keyed up for her as she was for him. And damn, he looked even better in faded jeans and a T-shirt than he did in a suit. Freer, more relaxed.

Well, maybe not exactly relaxed, given the furrowed brow and dark, searching gaze, but still.

She twisted her fingers together and cleared her throat.

"The diamond?" she asked, positive that wasn't the question that had been on the tip of his tongue.

He pointed to the middle of his broad chest, and her brain short-circuited for a second. Whoa. That was a hell of a lot of acreage he had there. And yes, she would like to touch that spot. In fact, she had touched it — kissed it, too — one incredible night not too long ago.

He kept his thumb on his shirt, where a pendant might have from a necklace. "The diamond."

"Oh, that diamond." She snapped back from her fantasies, and her words came out all barked and bitter as she pictured her precious family heirloom stuck between Elvira's fake boobs.

Tanner stuck his hands up, signaling something like, *Whoa. Just asking.* Either she was as transparent as the broth of her soup or the man could read her like a book.

"You said it belonged to your family," he prompted.

She stared down at her bowl, studying the scallion floating in the soup, wondering if she dared explain. Wondering if she could keep herself together if she did.

Tanner reached over, tipped her chin up gently, and offered her a crooked smile that said, *It'll be okay. It will be all right.* Like he really, truly understood all her worries, her insecurities, her fears.

The man's gaze was magic. And his touch... She could float away on it. Float away into the kind of dream she would never, ever want to end.

"It's not really dragon soup, is it?" he joked, breaking the tension in the room.

She shook her head and pulled herself together. "Nah. Just hot and sour soup."

He motioned over one bulky shoulder. "Do you know the people who run this place?"

An easier topic than everything else they had to cover, thank goodness.

"Distant cousins on my mother's side," she said between sips of soup. The dragons of old Europe and those of the Orient had remained separate for thousands of years, but there'd been occasional mixing, too.

"Your dragon side, you mean?" he asked quietly.

Karen froze with the spoon halfway to her mouth. Shit, had he figured out her other half?

She studied the eyes that studied her, dark and deep and, yes, a little wary. The world was full of shifter species, and though some developed rivalries, most accepted one another. Witches, though, were seen as outsiders — as different, the way vampires were.

Her chin dipped. Did he really want to hear her family history? Yikes, it looked like he did. She decided on the short version and resolved to keep emotion out of it.

"My mother is a dragon. Her first mate was a dragon, too, and they had my sister, Kaya."

Tanner nodded but didn't say a word. Barely breathed, it seemed.

"But he was killed in a battle, and a few years later, my mom, well... She hooked up with a warlock for a little while. My father."

Tanner's inscrutability terrified her, but she plunged on. Surely he wouldn't reject her for parentage she couldn't control?

"The dragon half of the family refused to accept him, and eventually, he left." She forced her voice to be steady as she tried to skip over the bitterest memories. Her mother's tears, her father's angry glare when he'd left. The loneliness she'd felt as an outsider in her own family. The only one who'd loved her unconditionally was her mother's father, the wisest, kindest dragon who had ever lived. He was the one who encouraged summer visits to her father, saying, *Family is family* and, *Who knows? You might learn a thing or two.*

And she had learned. A hell of a lot, in fact, though she'd never had the propensity for magic the way her witch-folk cousins had, just as she'd never had the full powers of her dragon kin.

Jack of all trades. Her grandfather would smile and pat her head.

She used to tack a few bitter words on under her breath. *Master of none.* She couldn't fly, and she was only a second-rate witch. What good was that?

The spoon shook in her hand, so she put it down. Slammed it down, practically, and closed her eyes, trying to ignore the voices that taunted her in her head.

You can't even fly.

You can't even do a proper spell.

You're a mutt, you know that?

Then something warm and strong closed over her hand, and all those thoughts turned tail and fled.

"Hey." Tanner stroked her skin with his thumb, looking at her in a completely new way.

She blinked until the scratchy sensation in her eyes went away. Then she rattled on with the story like an out of control train, because words were better than tears, right?

"I spent some time with my grandfather before he died, and he told me all the old dragon stories." There were hundreds of them, stretching back over eons, back to the beginning of time. Tales of knights and castles and battles fought and won. Tales of great prizes and brave deeds. As she spoke, she fought to stay focused because it was all too easy to picture long winter nights in a cabin with Tanner and a crackling fire, where she could recount all of those stories from beginning to end.

"My grandfather only saw the Blood Diamond once — as a child, before it was stolen by vampires in World War II. He said his only regret was that he'd never been able to track it down."

"Blood Diamond?" Tanner's eyebrows went up. "I thought that was a vampire thing."

She snorted. "They wish. The name comes from the story that the dragon who found it originally washed it with a drop of her own blood. That's what gave it that special tint and that shine." She nearly squinted, picturing the gem when she'd held it up to the moonlight in Schiller's penthouse. The brightest, clearest, most precious diamond she'd ever seen.

"I spent a long time researching the Blood Diamond, trying to track it down. And for ages, I came up with nothing." She leaned forward on her elbows. "Until one day, out of nowhere, I came across an ad for an auction."

Tanner pointed at her as if he knew exactly what she was talking about. "The auction here in Vegas a month ago?"

"Exactly. An auction advertising incredible riches brought to light for the first time."

"Including the Blood Diamond."

"Including the Blood Diamond." She nodded. "So I came out here, trying to see it. To verify it. I even snuck into the auction viewing—"

"Of course, you did." He sighed.

"And when I saw it..." She trailed off, stirring her hands in the air as if the diamond were right there, pulsing with power only a dragon could sense. "I knew that was really it."

She didn't say, *And I knew I had to have it,* because it wasn't about greed. It was about family pride. About righting a wrong. About proving herself.

"I didn't want it for me. I wanted to bring it back to dragonkind. To give them its power instead of letting vampires strut it around like another expensive toy. I was going to give it to the dragon elders, not keep it for myself."

"Why?"

"Why? To prove what I could do instead of demonstrating what I couldn't do. To finally have them accept me and value what I could do. To... to..." She stammered for a while, and her shoulders shook until Tanner closed his hand over hers and anchored her again.

She inhaled sharply and stared into her soup. Wow. Had she ever rammed as many sentiments into one breath? Had she ever admitted as much to herself?

Tanner let a minute tick by without saying anything. His fingers caressed hers while the candle on the table flickered, sending shadows over their hands.

"I swear I would have given it to the elders," she whispered.

"Of course, you would." He said it with such conviction, such unwavering faith, like it was self-evident and not a minor miracle.

Bears had honor, she knew. Bears like him, she could trust. The question was, would he trust her?

"Then Schiller bought it." Tanner gestured for her to continue.

She shook her head. "He *faked* buying it when, in fact, he was the owner the whole time. That part was hidden, of course, so he could pose as a buyer. It was all a publicity stunt to draw attention to the casino." It had cost her a couple of hundred bucks to bribe the truth out of a snake shifter who worked for the auctioneer.

Tanner nodded, disgust written all over his face. "That fits Schiller perfectly. The bastard."

"His family stole the diamond from mine, and the auction was all a front. The high price he paid drove up the prices on all the other diamonds in the auction and brought a lot of new customers to the casino. It allowed him to take the diamond out of whatever vault he had it locked away in and show it without being asked too many questions about where he obtained it. And then the bastard had the nerve to stick my family heirloom between Elvira's tits."

Tanner scowled as if the image disturbed him as much as it disturbed her.

Still, he sounded doubtful. "So you decided to steal it?"

"Okay, okay, that might not have been the best plan. But I had to do something. And it's not like I could outbid the Count of fucking Transylvania at his own game. Nineteen million, he paid for it."

Tanner scratched his chin thoughtfully. "Nineteen point two."

"You were there?" she yelped.

He nodded, and she nearly shoved the table. "You were at the auction? You stood by and let Count Fangula buy what rightfully belongs to me?"

He put up his hands in that, *Hey, I'm a good guy move* he did so well. "I didn't know it was yours. I didn't know you."

They stared at each other for a second while a thousand emotions collided in her heart and mind. Anger. Lust. Betrayal. Love. Hope. Bitter defeat.

"What are you doing working for those jerks, anyway?" she managed to shoot out.

He opened and closed his mouth a few times, then looked at his soup. "It's a long story."

"Summarize," she shot back.

He looked at her, and for the first time ever, he looked doubtful, even ashamed.

"I'll tell you." His voice was a little hoarse as he studied everything in the room but her. "While you eat. I have the feeling this is going to be a long night."

Chapter Eleven

Tanner puffed out his cheeks, then forced down some soup. His appetite had pretty much disappeared when Karen brought up Schiller, his boss. His goddamned vampire boss. Dammit, how did he ever agree to this gig?

He paused, tripping up on his own words. He was a bear working for a vampire. Crap. What did that make him look like?

And right there, he realized he should know better than to jump to hasty conclusions about a person. Maybe Karen being half witch didn't matter that much. The heart was what mattered, right?

The heart. His bear nodded. *The soul.*

He looked deep into her eyes and nearly drifted away there. It took a mental shake to force himself back to her question. Why was he working for bloodsuckers, again?

"Schiller's holding company—" he started.

Karen cut him off with a snort.

"Scarlet fucking Enterprises?"

He nodded. "They're expanding, even as far as Idaho. My bear clan caught wind of their latest project up there."

The elderly waitress cut into the conversation, swapping their soup bowls for food platters and trundling out again.

"Let me guess," Karen said as he took a bite of beef. "Another casino?"

"Yep. One they wanted to put smack in the middle of a stretch of pristine woods that borders our land. We saw the plans. They want to market it as some kind of get-in-touch with nature place."

"Sure," Karen snorted. "In touch with nature, like Vegas is? You can't even tell if it's day or night here, much less breathe fresh air."

Don't I know it, his bear sighed.

"We thought that land was an untouchable reserve but it turns out the deed is being disputed by a Native group." He put air quotes around the last two words.

"How Native?"

He shook his head. "About as Native as Schiller is."

"So what's the connection?"

"Schiller's men found some guy who's one-thirty-second Native — just enough to count — paid him off, and bankrolled the campaign to win the rights to the land."

"How about you buy off this guy instead?"

"We tried, but we can't match Schiller's offer."

"Which is?"

"Six million dollars."

Karen whistled, but Tanner just grimaced. His clan was rich in things that really counted — fresh air, clean water, and thick woods. Cash reserves, on the other hand, were pretty slim. And the last thing they needed was a group of vampires running a casino next door. The forest that buffered theirs would be cut down, and there would be outsiders all over the place. Outsider humans and, worse, vampires, who seemed to bring their own brand of organized crime everywhere they went.

"Isn't there some other way around it?"

He nodded. Thank goodness for that. "There's another guy — an owl shifter who's a genuine Native — who's been trying to protect that land for years as a preserve. If he finds enough money to take the case to court, we know he'll beat Schiller's guy. The land will stay wild, and the vampires will stay the hell away."

"So what's the problem?"

He scoffed. "Do you have a million dollars to spare?"

Karen leaned back in her chair, and his bear moaned a little, seeing the space between them open up again.

"Wow. Okay. Maybe not." She leaned forward again, and his bear rejoiced. "So you came to Vegas to... ?"

He forked a piece of beef a little more viciously than he meant to. "My clan sent me. The elders had this idea of somehow winning enough of Schiller's money to undermine him at his own game."

Karen grinned. "There is a beauty to that, I have to say."

"They assigned me the job of infiltrating Schiller's operation and setting something up."

"Something? Like what?"

He chewed another mouthful and washed it down with a swig of Tsingtao beer, buying time. Could he trust Karen with his secret?

She trusts us, his bear said. *We can trust her.*

But it wasn't that easy, was it?

Sure it is, his bear said. *Just make it easy.*

Man, he could see the look on the faces of the clan elders if he came home to say he'd not only fucked things up, but he'd done so after blurting secrets to a woman he barely knew.

"How about we eat first? Not because I don't trust you," he added quickly.

"No?" She glared at him and pointed her fork. "Then why not tell me?"

He bit his lip. "Because I don't trust myself."

"What's not to trust?"

He snorted. What wasn't to trust? Instinct. Emotion. Deviation from the original plan. Plus his bear, who kept insisting this woman was his mate. If he didn't watch it, he would be on his knees with an engagement ring in no time.

Karen regarded him in a way that said she didn't understand what about him was not to be trusted, which scared the crap out of him. Having the clan trust him to pull off the impossible was bad enough. Having a gorgeous dragon shifter trust him, too...

A good thing that busybody of a waitress bustled in then, this time with a baby panda on her hip.

"Aren't you a cutie?" Karen cooed, petting its ears.

Tanner expected his bear to get all jealous at that, but the grizzly inside him turned to mush.

So cute, the bear murmured. *And someday—*

Whoa, buddy, Tanner cut the bear off with a long, hard slug of his drink. *One thing at a time, all right?*

And just like that, his focus zoomed right in on Karen. Her sparkling eyes, her mile-a-minute lips making baby sounds, her silky hair. Everything else ceased to exist, and it was just the two of them again.

He would end up telling her, of course. He knew already he would. Every last detail of his plan — and the fact that it was going down tomorrow, and where and how. The whole truth and nothing but the truth, so help him God, because there was no way he could lie to his mate.

His half-dragon, half-witch mate. Boy, would he have a lot of explaining to do if he made it back to Idaho alive.

Daunting as that was, though, he warmed at the idea.

This is Karen, he would say, holding her close while he introduced her to his family. *My mate.*

His bear nodded his approval and practiced the throaty growl he would let out if any fool tried protesting such a crazy match.

My destined mate.

It kind of had a ring to it.

When the old lady took their dishes and left, Karen tilted her head at him. "You should see your expression right now. What are you thinking about?"

"You," he murmured. "You."

She reached over the table, took his hand in hers, and ran her fingers over his. Her skin was soft and nice and warm, and he couldn't help but close his eyes.

"What are you thinking of now?" she asked very quietly.

"Touching you," he whispered.

A silent second ticked by, and then she whispered back. "Where?"

And, *whoosh!* The little inner flames that had been flickering with lust for her throughout the past hour suddenly blazed into a giant inferno.

"Everywhere," he answered truthfully as his jeans grew tight.

A slow, sultry minute ticked by, and a bead of sweat formed on his brow as Karen undressed him with her eyes.

"And what else?" Her husky voice made his his blood heat.

"I'm thinking of kissing you. Everywhere." He imagined exactly where he would start — on the sweet spot just under her ear — and where he would go from there. Like the hollow of her neck, the curve of her collarbone, the rise of her breast. "I want to make love to you all night and all day."

She chuckled quietly. "You sure you mean me?"

Only you, his bear chipped in. *There is only you. No one else. Never.*

"You," he whispered, letting his thumb tango with hers.

"You and me?" Her voice became sultry. Hungry.

He nodded. "You and me."

His eyes were still closed, but he could picture the room. The silky wallpaper, the rich color of the red lamps overhead. Behind the smell of burning candles came the unmistakable scent of arousal. His and hers, wrapped around each other in the first steps of a very close samba. He took a deep breath.

"You and me..." Karen prompted, running her hand up his arm. Sparks shot through his body.

"You and me, together, like that night under the stars."

Her hand stayed on his while she stood from her chair, and it scraped against the floor. The space to his left warmed with her presence as her hand pulled slightly to the side. He pushed his chair back and let her slide into his lap. Smoothly, as if she'd done it a thousand times before. Eagerly, as if she wanted to do it a thousand more times, maybe even in front of a roaring fire in that log cabin he kept picturing whenever he thought ahead.

Her lips brushed over his, and she whispered softly in his ear. "You have that motorcycle somewhere nearby?"

His heart pounded harder. He nodded slowly, and her lips stayed on his ear, moving up and down, massaging his skin. Making every nerve in his body scream for her.

His arms slid around her — one around her waist, the other around her shoulders — without so much as a peek to guide him. His body knew hers instinctively. And when he opened his mouth to whisper, her lips were right there, so he couldn't tell if he started the kiss or she did. He didn't really care who it was, frankly, because a hundred delicious flavors filled his mouth and nose as he drank her in.

Beautiful, his bear murmured, already in ecstasy. *So beautiful.*

Karen squeezed closer. So close, her nipples pressed into his chest, about as erect as his cock inside his jeans. The buttons of that tight silk dress pressed against him, too, and he pictured popping them open, one at a time.

"Not sure I'll make it all the way to the bike and out to the hills," he murmured, letting his left hand curve over her ribs.

"Not sure I will, either." She kissed him down the side of his face to his neck and ran a hand inside his shirt.

The hand he'd been sneaking upward suddenly decided to go down, and he let it glide over her thigh, making her surge closer. Finding the hem of her dress, he tugged it higher. Higher. Higher...

"Tanner," she whispered.

A door opened and closed somewhere down the hall, and Tanner popped his head up, looking and listening.

"Don't stop," Karen begged, pushing his hand back to where it had been.

"Don't want to. But I really don't want Grandma Panda interrupting us now," he said, barely holding back. God, Karen was even more beautiful when she was turned on.

Slowly, she slid off his lap, wearing a sly smile. "I rented a room upstairs. A small room with a very big bed."

"Show me the way, sweetheart." He rose with her, keeping firm hold of her hand. "Show me the way."

Chapter Twelve

Karen led Tanner out of the room, down a hallway, and up a creaky set of stairs. She didn't make it far, though, before pausing for another kiss. A little taste of him to tide her over until they reached the privacy of her room.

Somehow, though, *quick* turned into *long* and *little* turned into *deep,* and she whimpered with the pleasure of it all. It only got better when Tanner pinned her against the wall with his big, hard body.

Her dragon purred inside. This kind of manhandling, she liked.

His hands tugged at the hem of her qípáo dress, and she congratulated herself on her choice of evening wear.

"You like this dress?" she murmured between kisses.

"I like this dress so much I need to take it off you very, very soon," he growled, pressing into another kiss. The firm line of his lips guided hers open, and his tongue plundered her mouth, exploring, celebrating, claiming all that territory as his.

A dozen alarms should have gone off in her mind, because everyone knew bears were the most territorial shifters of all. She really ought to be on guard against that. She was her own woman, after all.

But she'd had it with being her own. She wanted to be his. To let him consume her. Mark her. Claim her. She wanted to be part of a bonded twosome rather than the occasional one-plus-one. Even if it was only for tonight.

Not just for tonight, her dragon rumbled. *Forever.*

His body language all but screamed, *My woman,* and hers echoed the emotion back to him. Every rough scrape of his stubble over her cheek, every touch of his big hands wound her higher as he marked her with his scent.

I'm all yours, she told him through little gestures and touches. The message was coded into the way she rolled her head to the side, into the way she surrendered to his tongue, into the way she wound her leg around his.

His hips pushed against hers, and she climbed his leg like a boa.

"Here," he panted, hitching her leg higher. A second later, she was moaning incomprehensibly.

They were moving fast, but once the tidal wave of lust hit her, there was nothing to do but try to ride it out.

Not lust, her dragon corrected. *Love. This is my mate.*

"Mate?" she whispered, then winced. She hadn't meant to say it out loud.

Tanner's eyes shone with a deep, intense light, and he nodded. "Mate," he whispered back.

For a moment, she got lost there, gazing into his eyes as if they were crystal balls full of swirling mist that veiled her future. Then Tanner's mouth cracked open, and she dropped her head for another kiss. And another, and another, until the motion of him carrying her up the stairs rocked them apart.

"That one." She pointed to the door he nearly carried her past.

Tanner shoved it open with a foot then shouldered it shut without letting her go. From the looks of it, he might never let her go, and she was just fine with that.

She sniffed around his neck as he slid his hands lower, pushing her dress up and spreading her legs wider. Which was perfect, except for one thing.

"Too many layers," she mumbled, loosening her grip around his waist.

"Too many layers," he agreed.

Blue neon lights washed in from outside the windows, framing Tanner in a smoky glow. A group of tourists walked down the alley one story down, and a laugh rang out.

Tanner splayed one big hand over her ribs while running the knuckles of the other over the front of her dress.

"Too many buttons."

She shook her head. "Just enough buttons, I think."

"Just enough for what?" The look he gave her was so scorching, she wavered a tiny bit.

"Enough to make this fun. I can always start if you want." She reached for the button of his jeans.

A deep, dangerous rumble sounded in his chest, and for a moment, she thought he would pounce.

"Start where?" His voice was low and rumbly, like thunder behind a mountain ridge.

"Right about here." She popped open the top button of his jeans and ran a finger up the line of the zipper, teasing him. Then she cupped him with one hand — a hand that was nowhere near big enough to hold everything straining the denim.

Just as she started to wonder why Tanner would let her take the lead, the answer came to her. A man with such intensity would have easily dominated every woman he'd ever touched. Maybe having her lead was a novelty. Maybe he liked it.

He definitely liked it, judging by the gleam in his eye, the hitch in his breath. The question was, how long would he let her run with it? How far could she push him?

All of a sudden, she really, really wanted to find out.

"Let me see," she said, though *seeing* wasn't what her hands were busy doing with his jeans. "How about you lose these?" She made it a command, not a request, and his nostrils flared.

She hurried on before he might intervene, unzipping the fly and slowly pushing down his jeans.

"Oops. Shoes," she murmured.

He reached for them, but she caught his hand.

"On second thought, leave them like that. I like you trapped. Helpless."

His right eyebrow arched. "Helpless?"

"Helpless," she replied. As helpless as a two-hundred-pound bear shifter could be, at least. Even if that wasn't much, she was having too much fun to stop now. "This way, I can proceed with my diabolical plan." She ran her hands down his chest, inching gradually south.

His body was tense, his eyes full of lust, and his mouth crooked in the slightest smile. "An actual plan?"

"Hey! I always have a plan."

He tilted his head, clearly skeptical.

"They just have a way of evolving as I go along."

"Evolving, huh?"

"Evolving." She nodded firmly. She slid her fingers down and found his cock jutting nearly straight up. "Of course, I can always stop," she threatened, dropping slowly, deliberately, to her knees.

Tanner looked down at her from what seemed to be ten feet above. "Don't stop." His voice was a hoarse whisper.

She leaned in, holding him, then turned her head and kissed the tip.

His whole body shuddered with barely restrained need, and he knotted his fingers in her hair.

"Don't stop," he whispered again.

Oh, she had no intention of that. She licked him all the way down and up one side then the other, and finally took him in her mouth. In no time, she found herself making little noises as she slid up and down. Taking him deeper, retreating, and rocking closer to take another inch. Her tongue lapped at the same time, and her whole body heated. Tanner's power seethed just below the surface, but for the moment, she was the one calling the shots. A high in itself with a man like him.

She set into a slow, steady rhythm while he clutched at her hair, at empty space, and at the smooth surface of the door he leaned against. She knew she would be grabbing for the sheets the same way when they moved to the bed, and making noises much louder than the hungry little pants Tanner let out as she worked him up and down. She swirled her tongue around the head of his shaft and let her lips tug, then opened wide and took him deeper still.

He whispered something, or maybe yelled it, but she wasn't tuned in to anything but the feel, the taste, the heat stirring her bones.

"Wait," he insisted, and the word dimly registered in her ears.

She slid slowly away, one millimeter at a time, and peered up. Nice view. All that bear, right there for the taking. Why stop now?

"No good?"

"Too good." He pulled her up and kissed her. Then he broke off to say something, but his eyes sparked first, as if he'd just registered the taste of himself on her lips. He dove back for more.

Karen slid his shirt up, playing with his nipples, aching for more contact.

Tanner panted against her neck for a second, every muscle straining at invisible bonds.

"I could finish what I started, you know," she murmured.

He shook his head. "The only place I want to come is in you."

Well, he had been in her, but she wasn't going to argue technicalities. Not with an offer like that.

"Well then, show me what you got."

He cupped her face in both hands and smoothed his thumbs down her cheeks, looking more serious than ever. Happily-ever-after kind of serious, which made her pulse skip. Then he cracked a tiny smile and pulled back. "Did your plan include getting my jeans off before my boots, or the other way around?"

She looked down, and of course, he was still tangled in his own clothes. Oops. "Minor detail."

A detail he rectified in ten seconds flat when he yanked his shirt and shoes off, followed by the jeans and his boxers.

All that man-flesh, naked to her eye. *Yum,* her dragon yowled.

Tanner backed her up to the bed one step at a time. "Just. Wait," he said, uttering one word with each slow step, "Til. You. See. My. Plan."

"I'm not good at waiting." Her legs bumped the mattress. When he lowered her slowly, she hung on to the chiseled lines of muscle in his shoulders, refusing to let go.

"I noticed. But I'm not the one with all the buttons." He ran his knuckles down her silk dress as he had before. Down, then up, bumping over each knot button, rising over the swell of her breasts, and dipping toward her waist.

"So get to work, mister." She slid her hand down his naked belly.

He caught her before she reached too low and guided her hand to his shoulder. "This belongs here. And this," he said, leading her left hand to his neck, "belongs here."

Ah, the bear was taking charge again. Well, she could go with the flow.

"And you belong here." She guided his lips to hers.

His kisses worked her into a whimpering mess with tricks of the tongue that had to be a special bear thing — and wow, what a thing — before starting on a long, winding path along her body.

"I belong here," he whispered, kissing her neck.

Her body lifted when his teeth scraped over the sensitive skin, and a groan escaped her lips.

"And here." As he kissed his way over to the other side, one knot button after another surrendered to his nimble fingers, and the tight dress grew looser around her chest.

"Getting the hang of them now," he murmured, rushing through the last few. The buttons slid free of the loops holding them. Even then, it took some work to pull the form-fitting dress off, but that was nothing compared to what she'd gone through to put it on. But it had all been worth it, because when he stripped her of her bra and panties and laid her back down, his jaw had a hard set to it and his eyes a feral glow.

Mine, those eyes said as he came down over her body. *All mine.*

She nearly echoed him, but his lips caught her nipple and she cried out instead.

Oh, this is going to be good, her dragon hummed inside.

Leaning back to let the man do the work had never felt so good, so fast. Tanner consumed her. Feasted on her. Sandpapered her most sensitive spots with his stubbly chin. The soft undersides of her breasts, her belly, her inner thighs. He worked her with his fingers and tongue, winding her higher and higher.

Her hair was probably a mess, her body sweaty, her face contorted with happy cries. She'd never felt so good or so thoroughly, deliciously ravished. He went at her like a bear might go at honey after a long winter's sleep, and all she could do was moan and wind her limbs around his.

"More," she mumbled every time he ignited a new set of nerves in her body. Nerves she didn't know she had before. Nerves that seemed to have been slumbering all her life before jumping into action now.

"More," he agreed, nudging her legs apart with a knee.

She felt like a one-woman slot machine. *Zing-zing-zing!* No matter how Tanner touched her, the reels would line up, making her a winner again and again.

They didn't bother with a condom because shifters had nothing to worry about except making babies, and she wasn't in heat.

Good Lord, what a thought, her dragon sighed. If she was this desperate for him now, how mindless with lust would she feel when she was in heat?

Tanner popped his head up and stared. Had he heard her thoughts?

Her mind drifted with burning images while his eyes flared.

First things first, sweetheart.

Whoa. She could hear his voice in her head? He had to be her mate. According to legend, the truest of destined mates could hear each other's thoughts before they traded mating bites if they trusted one another enough.

Trust. Yikes. Did she really dare?

Of course, we dare, her dragon chided. *And of course, he's our mate.*

Of course, I'm your mate, his bear echoed.

"Then show me." She extended her arms over her head, giving herself over to him as she'd never given herself to any man before. Then she closed her eyes to the sweet, slow burn of him sliding into her. "Yes."

81

Tanner pulled back, thrust forward, and opened his mouth in a silent exclamation. Each time he pulled back, her soul sobbed in protest. Each time he hammered in, her heart cried in relief. She bucked her hips in time with his, and when he pulled her knees higher along his waist, she cried out again.

"So good..." Nothing she said could capture the sensation, though she didn't stop trying. "God, yes..."

The bed creaked, and the water in the glass she'd left on the side table earlier threatened to splash right over the rim. Tanner huffed harder and pushed deeper while she tilted her head farther and farther back, focused entirely on the fire building within her. A fire that grew and grew and grew until she was howling for release.

"Tanner," she cried.

He rocked harder. Deeper. Faster, until his whole body went stiff and a groan slipped past his lips.

Karen hit her climax a second later, shuddering as wave after wave of pleasure coursed through her veins. She hung on to him, lost to all sense of time and place. Lost to everything but the feel of her man. His cock, buried deep, deep inside her. His heart, pounding against hers. His sweet breath, warming her neck.

He lowered his body until it was flush with hers, and in the brief pauses between each of his panting breaths, she heard him whisper her name.

"Karen..."

Music to her ears. His voice was pure music to her ears.

Chapter Thirteen

Tanner's bear made him mumble Karen's name as he held her tight.

"My mate," he whispered, pressing his lips to her skin.

He was through denying it. There was no way Karen could be anything but his mate. He'd never hungered after a woman as much before. He'd never spent so much time marveling at a woman's eyes, voice, or laughter before. He'd never gone from rock hard to jelly as quickly, and he sure as hell had never listened to his bear sing like a happy drunk.

Mine! My mate!

So, okay, he got it already. Karen was his destined mate.

Isn't she amazing? his bear hummed.

He let out a slow breath and hugged her closer. Yes, she was amazing. Funny. Unique. And she drove him crazy in the very best way. So what if she was occasionally a little headstrong and got herself into trouble?

He caught himself there. Karen was always headstrong, and she always got into trouble. Could he live with that?

Can we live without that? his bear kicked in.

No, he couldn't. But if only she weren't quite so reckless...

His bear shrugged. *Then she wouldn't be the one I love.*

He traced the delicate line of her collarbone with a finger. The thing was, she could be so stubborn, too.

Stubborn can be good, his bear decided.

What about impulsive?

If she weren't impulsive, we would never have met her. We never would have taken her out that night.

Damn, his bear had a point. Just the thought of having missed her, of going through life ignorant of his destined mate, hurt to consider.

Still, it would be easier if she weren't so damned unpredictable.

His bear grinned inside, so much that his human cheeks moved with the gesture. *Predictable is boring. Chalk it up to a more interesting life.*

All his life, he'd been taught to be careful. To think things through. To lay plans and foundations and build upon them, one cautious step at a time. And yeah, it worked.

But damn, could life be dull that way.

Her bare skin took on the blue tint of the neon light outside. He stroked her shoulder, marveling at the contradiction of it all. The situation couldn't be crazier or more uncertain, and yet he'd never felt so calm or satisfied or content. He even felt safe, which was nuts, because she was a witch. A fugitive. A thief.

"Hey," she murmured, turning in his arms, coming face-to-face.

And there it was again, that stab of emotion, that hallelujah chorus, those fireworks in his chest.

"Hey," he whispered back.

"You're blue." She smiled, running a finger along his cheek.

He grinned in spite of himself. "So are you. And anyway, the only color I'm fed up with is red."

She nestled closer, mesmerizing him. Her eyes were shining the way they had at the diamond, and his heart beat a little faster. He'd heard about dragons and their lust for treasures. But to be counted in that category?

Wow.

She nodded solemnly. "Mate. My destined mate."

He let a second or two tick by, digesting her easy acceptance of that crazy fact.

"I wasn't sure dragons believed in that," he murmured.

Karen snuggled along his shoulder and neck, and his bear sighed happily inside.

"Some do, some don't. I didn't really believe it until now." She kissed him. "No telling with dragons sometimes."

"What about witches?"

She tensed. "Why do you ask?"

He shifted around so she could see the truth in his eyes. The worry — and the hope, too. "There's been a lot of bad blood between bears and witches where I come from."

She sighed, and the sound had a bitter note. "There's a lot of bad blood between witches and shifters in lots of places. It's not my fault."

He tipped her chin up when she dipped it. The last thing he wanted was to derail things now. "I'm not saying it is. I'm just trying to figure things out."

"Like what?" Her voice was tight.

Like how to screw up this perfect night? His bear shook its head at him.

"Like how I'll beat it into my clanmates' heads that you're mine."

She broke into a smile, and her muscles loosened up again. "You would do that for me?"

I would die for you, his bear swore solemnly.

"I would do anything for you."

She stared at him a long while then nodded. "So, ask. Ask me anything you want to know."

He pulled her closer because the inch of space that had opened up between them was way too much.

"How much witchcraft do you know?"

She made a face. "Some spells, I'm really good at. Others, not so much."

"Fire spells, for example?" He crooked an eyebrow, remembering the damage on the twenty-seventh floor.

She flashed a naughty smile and gave him a thumbs-up.

"Invisibility?"

She snorted. "I wish."

"Mind control?" He gripped the bedpost a little too hard.

She laughed outright, and he let the subject go. Maybe the witch part didn't have to be scary. No scarier than it had to be for her to face a guy who could turn into a grizzly. And

85

yet she hadn't asked any paranoid questions, like whether he hibernated — God, no — or ate honey straight from the comb — hell, yes — or whether he liked to rake his claws down trees.

He thought it all over one more time, then put it to rest forever. So, she was half witch. So what? She was his mate.

"How long have you been planning the diamond heist?" He knew how tight security was in the building. Karen, with her unique mix of dragon and witch abilities, might be the only person on earth who could pull off that break-in.

She looked at him blankly. "What do you mean, how long?"

"Well, I've been working on this inside job for months now—"

"Months?" She gaped. That she was the spontaneous type, he'd figured out.

"Well, some things take time."

"Some things take luck," she countered.

Now he was the one gaping. "Luck?" He thought it over. When had he ever left anything to luck?

Karen nodded firmly.

He stared. "Your plan to steal the diamond was to get lucky?"

She made a face. "I had a plan. It just needed some tweaking."

He wondered whether she'd started tweaking in midair on her flight to the casino roof or sometime later on.

Finally, she shrugged. "What can I say? Sometimes it's good to be impulsive."

"Like when?" He sat up, reaching for the water glass by the bed.

"Like the first night we met," she said with a sultry grin. "Like just now. 'Cause I sure didn't see blow jobs on the menu downstairs."

He choked, spraying water everywhere, and his dick twitched. "Okay, maybe being impulsive is good in some ways."

"Admit it," she teased, sitting up and tickling him. "Being spontaneous is good. Being childish can be fun."

He tried to roll away, but she was too quick, and before he knew it, his bear was giggling wildly, some of which made it past his lips.

"Repeat after me," Karen said, looking wild and innocent and free. "I will try to be impulsive for once in my life."

"I will try..." he started, then broke out laughing again.

Karen plowed right on, tickling mercilessly. "I will trust luck and love and let my wild side out."

Luck, he wasn't so sure about. Love, one hundred percent. And letting his wild side out?

Already happening, his bear pointed out as the tickling continued, along with the chuckles he couldn't hold back.

"I will trust crazy dragons," she continued.

"I will trust crazy dragons," he sputtered as he rolled on the mattress.

"I will live and laugh and make love."

A no-brainer. "I will live and laugh and make love," he repeated. "To you."

She grinned like a Cheshire cat.

"Hey! Don't stop!" he protested, even though he had a pillow clutched to his stomach and his arms up like a fence. He hadn't been tickled since he was a cub, and that was a damn shame.

"Do you know how hard it is to tickle through this much muscle?" She smacked his belly.

"Well then, there's always an alternative way to have fun." He sat up and pulled her closer.

"See? Spontaneous." She smiled, sliding her arms around his neck. "I think you're getting the hang of this at last."

He guided her legs around his sides so the two of them sat face-to-face, intertwined and gazing into each other's eyes.

"I think I do," he said, more seriously.

She pressed closer, and he slid his hand slowly down between them.

"Oh, you definitely have the hang of this."

She sighed as he ran a finger through her folds. She was already warm and slick and ready for more. A minute of exploring later, he was lined up just right, and his cock slid home.

His eyes closed with the soaring sensation that went through his veins, then he forced them open again, determined to capture the moment in every possible way.

"Yes..." Karen tipped her head back as he penetrated, and her pulse beat visibly on her neck. Exactly the spot where he would place his mating bite someday.

Someday soon, his bear said.

"More," she breathed, looking at him through half-lidded eyes. "Harder."

Harder wasn't easy in a seated position, but he did his damned best. Holding her hips, watching her breasts jiggle, finding just the right angle. She was tight and hot and perfect in every way. His breath was already speeding out of control, his body burning, his cock straining...

"Yes..." Karen rolled her head to the side, subconsciously offering him a place to bite.

Yes, his bear growled.

Every instinct screamed at him to lean forward, but he forced himself to do the opposite. It was too soon for that, even if he was certain she was his mate.

Can never be too soon, his bear complained.

Damn bear was in such a rush. There was pleasure in patience, too. Pleasure in watching his mate come undone. He held her with one hand while the other toyed with the taut nipple that pointed upward, a mere inch away from the sweat glossing his chest.

"Yes..."

He rocked his hips and pulled her closer still. Catching her reflection in the mirror to one side, he turned his head to watch her move in time with him. In perfect time, like they'd been made for each other.

We are made for each other, his bear huffed past another heavy groan.

Her legs tightened around his waist. Her nails scraped his back.

"Tanner!" she cried, about to let it all go.

He rocked harder, gritting his teeth. Holding back his own high until Karen came too. His breath came in sharp pants and crazy little grunts as he pounded into her with everything he had.

Mark our woman, his bear chanted. *Fill her. Claim her.*

She leaned her upper body far, far back, but he kept her hips good and close. Her firm, peaked breasts swayed as their bodies rocked.

Her lips curled back from her teeth, and her eyes shone as she shuddered, coming around him.

"Yes..." she mumbled through her orgasm.

His bear was no better, moaning the same words inside his mind. The wave that had been building inside him rushed forward as he delivered one final thrust, groaning with the pleasure-pain of release. Her arms shook as he emptied inside her, and he clutched her close.

Deep was one of the few clear thoughts in his mind. *Close* was another. *Mine,* too.

Karen went soft all over as he went hard, and his bear nearly whimpered in joy at the perfect match they made.

Amazing. She's amazing, the beast hummed as he slowly descended from his high.

He held her flush against his chest to feel her ribs rise and fall with each beat of her racing heart.

"Oh..." Karen squeaked and threw her head back as an aftershock raked her body.

He tightened his grip again, savoring the sight. It was one thing to make a woman feel good. It was even better when that feeling sparked a thousand emotions and made him glow, too.

You're amazing, his bear murmured in his head.

"You, too," Karen whispered back.

Tanner froze. Right, she could hear his thoughts. That proved that their animal sides had already bonded.

His bear leaned back with a smug grin. *You think I need to bite to make her mine?*

Karen laughed, and he could hear the throaty voice of her dragon echo the words. *I sure don't need a bite to know this bear is mine.*

They sat slumped against each other, panting while their shifter sides crooned about love, destiny, undying devotion, and all kinds of things that had never occupied his mind before, though they were all he could think about now.

Forever, his bear vowed as he nuzzled her cheek.

Forever, her dragon agreed, and she wound her leg around his.

Dang, he was a goner. And he wouldn't want it any other way.

They unwound just far enough to flop to the mattress, letting time tick by without caring whether it was minutes or hours they spent there.

"Now, about this plan of yours," Karen said at one point.

He groaned. "Maybe we can talk shop tomorrow."

She ran her fingers along his collarbone, making his bear hum. "I was thinking we should make a plan."

He did have a plan. It was just that she'd nearly blown it to smithereens.

"I think we should leave that for tomorrow," he suggested.

Her eyebrows shot up. "Oh, you mean like a spur of the moment? Spontaneous? Maybe even reckless?" Her eyes had a definite gleam.

He rolled, pinning her body under his, and grinned. "I might just be getting the hang of that, you know."

She hooked a leg around him, pressing her hips closer, and just like that, he was on fire again.

"Then show me, bear. Show me."

Chapter Fourteen

The colors of the setting sun competed with the lights of Las Vegas Boulevard. Tourists crowded the sidewalks, headed for various spectacles. The pirate show at Treasure Island, the Volcano at the Mirage, and the sound and light show of the Scarlet Palace, where red lights illuminated dozens of fountains, giving the impression of bubbling blood.

Karen stood by a corner of one of the pools, trying to settle her pulse. But who was she kidding? Her heart had started hammering when she'd been six blocks away, and it was only getting worse.

"Aren't they beautiful?" a woman sighed to her partner as she dipped a hand in at the water's edge.

Sure, if you like gushing blood, Karen wanted to say.

"Like roses," the woman went on. "Like red wine."

Like a vampire's best fantasy, Karen nearly blurted, but she squeezed her mouth shut.

"I think this is going to be our lucky night," the man said, stroking the woman's hair.

Karen fingered the wad of bills in her right pocket and nodded to herself. It sure as hell better be her lucky night, because heading back into the Scarlet Palace had to be one of the more suicidal things she'd ever done.

Maybe bears were right. Maybe she ought to consider a more cautious approach.

They'll never recognize us, her dragon murmured inside.

She readjusted the gold-rimmed glasses on her nose and patted her hair. The vampires had better not recognize her. She'd spent an hour teasing her hair into three times its usual volume and practicing a toothy smile unlike her own. It would have been so much easier to carry a little cloaking spell around with her, but the casino would be on high alert after her recent break-in, and she couldn't risk any unnecessary magic that might be sensed by the vampire's witches-for-hire.

Third-rate witches, her dragon sniffed.

She made a face, because the most she could claim to be was a second-rate witch. Second-rate witch, second-rate dragon—

Stop that! her dragon barked.

Well, it was true.

I'll prove it to you sometime, the dragon declared.

She sighed. Let the beast live its little fantasies. Let it think what it wanted about a someday that would never come. She was still second-rate, no matter what it claimed.

Got myself a first-rate mate, the dragon hummed.

That part was true. A night with Tanner had only cemented it all in her mind. He was hers, and she was his. Forever.

That is, if they survived this crazy crusade. Much as she and Tanner had tried to bullet-proof their plan, a lot could go wrong. Too much could go wrong. Any of a dozen different scenarios could end with her as a captive of the vampires — worse still, as a blood donor to her least favorite cause. Now that the vampires suspected she was only half dragon, they would all vie for the first sip of her blood.

The last sip, too.

Her skin crawled, imagining them pinning her down and sinking their teeth into her neck. Or maybe two at her neck and another two at her wrists. The very worst was the idea of Schiller, forcing her head to the side and stepping close. Licking his lips to taunt her and looking her right in the eye with that *I knew you'd be mine* look. Schiller would prolong her death just to toy with her, like a cat with a mouse.

She shivered, trying to push thoughts of disaster away. Tanner said it was all taken care of. Schiller would be out of the casino until at least midnight at a meeting with his business associates, the Westend wolves. Which left her three hours to win and win big.

"Definitely gonna be our lucky night," the woman said, walking toward the entrance of the Scarlet Palace.

Karen forced herself to follow the couple, clutching her purse close. The two thousand dollars in her pocket was peanuts compared to what she had in her bag, because she'd spent the day going from one small casino to another, raking up modest wins that would fall under the radar of casino security. Five thousand here, seven or eight thousand there. All it took was a tiny flick of her fingers just as the reels of a slot machine clicked into position or the split second before a roulette ball fell. She could risk little bursts of magic as long as she stuck to small bets in human-run establishments around town.

And it had worked. The ten thousand dollars she'd started with had multiplied to over one hundred thousand — enough to set the main part of Tanner's plan into motion.

She tilted her head back and looked past all the glittering windows and lights of Vegas to the stars emerging in the indigo sky. One last look at freedom, one last gulp of fresh air—

Someone jostled her, and she stumbled inside.

"Sorry, honey." A man grabbed her elbow to steady her.

She was so on edge, she nearly flashed her dragon fangs.

"No problem." She faked a smile.

If nothing else, the little push had rushed her past the bouncers stationed at the doors without a second glance.

"How about I make it up to you with a drink at the bar?" the man offered. He was bald and short and smelled like so many other humans in Vegas — a blend of hope and despair, half hidden behind his cheap cologne. But she figured he would make good cover, so she played along.

"Sure." She nodded, taking the elbow he offered.

If it had been Tanner at her side, she would have felt like a million bucks. Women would turn their heads with jealous looks, and men would move aside to make way for Tanner's bulk. She entertained herself with that little fantasy all the way to the mezzanine-level bar. The place overlooked the gambling floor where she spotted Tanner making his rounds. Just seeing him settled the butterflies fluttering inside her.

"I love this place." The man pointed at the bar sign. "Bloody Mary's."

Karen rolled her eyes.

"What will it be, honey?"

She wasn't this human's honey, and she wasn't in the mood for a drink with anything red in it, so she ordered a tequila with lime and suffered through his conversation while checking out the scene below.

Semicircular tables took up most of the floor space in the blackjack hall. Mirrors covered the walls, making the room look twice its actual size. She leaned right, trying to catch a glimpse of the corner Tanner had told her about, but she couldn't quite spot it.

It's the only table in the whole place that only has one camera on it, he'd explained back in the hotel room, where they'd lain skin to skin, formulating a plan.

The way the mirrors were angled made it perfect, too. Tanner had scoped it out himself. The only mirror that might have reflected their target table to another camera or pair of eyes had been taken out to widen a service door.

Karen's eyes darted over the tables as a chant went through her mind.

Will not screw this up. Cannot screw this up. Not like last time.

"You planning to play the slots tonight, honey?" Her companion grinned at her through nicotine-stained teeth.

She held back a scowl. The slot machines had been her undoing three weeks ago, when she'd been fool enough to march into this very casino and try a little magic on them. The witch on duty had been a sharp one — sharp enough to sense the magic and to let Karen play just long enough to be nabbed with eighty thousand dollars she'd won illegally — illegally, that is, by the unwritten rules of the Scarlet Palace. When Schiller discovered she was a dragon, he'd locked her up and held her for ransom. Thank goodness for older sisters coming to the rescue, though even that had been a close call.

She licked salt off her knuckle, gulped her tequila, and sucked on a slice of lime, trying to replace one bitter taste with another. That was all in the past. Tonight was about the future, and man, she couldn't wait to put Vegas behind her.

When her companion took a swig of his own drink, she peeked at his watch. Already a quarter to eight?

"Well, thanks." She stood abruptly and stepped away from the table.

"What? Honey, we haven't even started to have fun."

She faked a sad smile. "Gotta go. Good luck." The man had helped her enter the casino unnoticed, but the last thing she needed was for him to hang around now that the arranged time was approaching. So she raced out of the bar before he could follow and waved to one of the women hovering by the balcony — one of many painted ladies looking for an easy ride for the night.

"The bald guy at the corner table isn't much to look at." Karen jabbed a thumb toward him. "But he has cash to burn tonight."

Her words were aimed at one woman, but three primped their hair and closed in on the bar.

Karen grinned, then pursed her lips. If only the rest of the night would be as easy. But it had only just begun.

Chapter Fifteen

"I'm in," Karen said to the dealer, sliding into the last free chair at the corner table before anyone else beat her to it.

The portly hedgehog shifter who'd just vacated the space winked on his way out, and Karen hid her smile.

Just like Tanner arranged. Her dragon nodded in satisfaction.

The dealer's eyes didn't so much as flicker, even though he was in on the arrangement, too. In fact, he was a key piece of the puzzle that had to align perfectly if she was going to make it out of the casino alive with a million dollars. The man's name tag said Dexter Davitt, but Tanner had called him Dex.

Find the corner table. The one where Dex deals, he'd said.

Dex?

The smile Tanner flashed was the only one he'd shown in the time they'd spent going over his plan. *Dex. A friend of mine.*

How will I recognize him?

Another grin. *Think Denzel Washington crossed with Brad Pitt.*

She'd had a hard time imagining that, but now, she understood. Dex had the smile and charm of the former plus the bright eyes of the latter. The standard-issue smile he shot her showed a row of perfect white teeth against his dark skin — enough to make two nearby women sigh. Karen might have drooled the way they did, too, if she hadn't already lost her heart to Tanner.

Tanner, who kept striding in and out of her vision if she peeked at just the right time. His job was to keep other security guards away. Hers was to work with Dex to win big.

Dex, the panther shifter. She looked at the man's impassive face. Tanner trusted the panther, so she would, too. Dex would earn a fifty percent cut of the winnings — a cool million of his own — if everything went right tonight. That meant she had to win two million to come away with enough for Tanner's clan after splitting the total with Dex.

And what about the Blood Diamond? her dragon asked.

That was the only part of the plan she disliked. *Hated* was more like it, but Tanner had been right about giving up on the diamond. It was too risky, and she was turning over a new leaf in her life. Swindling Schiller out of enough money to derail his Idaho casino deal would have to be reward enough — together with the reward of getting out alive with her mate.

So, focus, she reminded herself. *Focus!*

Dex sat across the table from her, making his casino uniform look like a finely tailored suit. On her right were two men: first, a human in jeans and an expensive leather jacket whose thick mustache would have given Freddie Mercury a run for his money. Beside him sat a penguin shifter — the scent and the tuxedo were a dead giveaway.

To Karen's left was a haughty brunette who looked about to bust out of her sheath dress. Her lips were painted so red, she was bound to pick up a vampire sooner or later.

It's not worth it, honey, Karen wanted to whisper, but she kept her mouth shut.

On the outer left sat a human in a somber suit who shook a couple of chips in his hand as if this was a craps game and not blackjack. The chips clinked against each other, driving Karen nuts. The final gambler was a woman in a black-and-white dress. Karen squinted and realized the pattern was made up entirely of little Elvis silhouettes, repeated in a dizzying pattern.

"Place your bets, ladies and gentlemen. Place your bets," Dex called.

Karen placed her chips on the table in neat stacks and took a deep breath. She didn't dare glance behind her to where Tanner said the sole camera aimed at Dex's table was placed. She bet two five-hundred-dollar chips, waited for the deal, checked her cards... and promptly lost.

Freddie Mercury pumped a fist. Elvis-girl squeaked. Karen pretended to look disappointed, because that was all part of the plan — to lose some, win some, until the moment came to win big.

Really big, her dragon added.

She blinked a few times to make sure her eyes didn't shine the way they did whenever her dragon saw riches, then placed another bet.

"Hit me," she said on the second round. With a nine and a three in her hand, she didn't really have a choice, not with the dealer showing a card that was unlikely to bust.

Dex obliged, sliding her another card, which she left face-down until he called the round.

"Damn," she muttered, flipping over an eight.

"Bust," the woman with the overdone lipstick sneered.

I'll show you bust, lady, her dragon muttered in her head.

Karen rearranged her stack of chips and bided her time. The skin on the back of her neck prickled as the space behind her filled with a feathery noise.

"Dex, honey, how long are you working tonight?" a woman's voice called.

All the men swiveled their heads around fast enough to risk whiplash, and when Karen turned, she saw why. A Vegas showgirl stood there, tall and practically topless but for the scraps of fabric covering her nipples. The plumage rising high from her headdress would have covered more than those tiny triangles with tassels on the ends.

The headdress is covering the security camera, too, Karen's dragon pointed out.

Her mate was a goddamn genius, bringing the showgirl in on this. A showgirl looking to earn a little bonus before she left Vegas for good, he'd said.

"Hi, Amber," Dex said. "I'm on for another hour, baby."

Her feathers were the perfect means to block the camera without drawing attention. And if Tanner was right, the security detail currently on duty was the slowest and laziest of the bunch. Chances of them noticing the blocked camera and hustling the showgirl along were slim.

"Too bad," Amber sighed. "I'll just watch for a few minutes."

Karen's pulse spiked, because there was a message coded into those words. *All set. Camera's blocked, but not for very long.*

It took everything she had not to lean forward eagerly and push every one of her chips into the betting box.

Bet small first, then build up, Tanner had told her, and it was his gig, so she did exactly as she was told, putting another thousand on the table. Dex made the briefest possible eye contact with her when he dealt, but his signal was clear. *One ace and one nine, coming right up.*

Nineteen to the dealer's ten. She waved her hand, rejecting a third card. "Stand."

She beat the house on that round, and the next, and the next, betting higher every time until she was playing the limit every round. She stayed just under the amount Dex was required to call in and obtain approval for, which would protect the dealer when all was said and done.

A bead of sweat formed on her brow. Time was ticking, and though she didn't dare count her chips, she knew she had close to eight hundred thousand dollars.

If Tanner had been at the table with her, he would have shaken his head. *Not enough. Especially since we need enough for us and enough for Dex.*

She tapped her fingers on the green felt of the table, wishing the other players would speed the hell up. The guy on her left kept sliding his chips around, making an agonizing decision about every bet. And no wonder, because he was losing. Red Lips lost a lot, too, which only made her toss down more of the pink cocktail in a glass now smudged with lipstick all the way around the rim. Somehow, that drove Karen crazy, too. Everything did except the cards she drew.

"Wow, two nines," the penguin shifter marveled at her next hand.

"Split," she murmured, trying to keep her cool while Dex dealt her a jack and an ace.

"Holy. . ." Freddie Mercury started.

"Double." Karen tapped her bet.

". . . shit," the man finished when the round closed for another win. "Two hands doubled at twenty-five thousand each. . ."

A cool hundred thousand in chips that Karen eagerly scooped closer to her chest.

All that money, her dragon hummed.

It was still too little, but it was adding up fast. After another two rounds, she started betting even higher. Dex reached under the table, just as Tanner said he would. Dealers were required to alert security to big bets and repeat winners — which would mean big trouble if Tanner hadn't snipped the wire in the communications room earlier. In the investigation that was sure to ensue, Dex could truthfully say he'd placed the call, even though it hadn't gone through.

Our mate is a genius, her dragon cooed.

She tapped the table with her knuckles, hurrying the next round up. Did the penguin really have to count and recount his chips with every hand? And did the woman at the end of the table have to hum Elvis songs?

Several rounds later, the feathers behind her rustled impatiently, and when Dex's eyes stopped on someone across the room, Karen froze. Was she out of time? Was security coming over to check out the action at her table?

Dex's shoulders relaxed the slightest bit, telling her the coast was clear, but he dealt the next round in double time.

Just a little longer. Her dragon gritted its teeth and all her muscles tensed.

Remember, even eight hundred thousand after we split it with Dex will do, Tanner had said. *We can figure out where to raise the rest.*

She ground her teeth. She didn't want to win just enough. She wanted every dollar Tanner needed to protect his clan's land. For him, and for her own sake, because it was another way of proving herself to Tanner and his family.

"Hit me," she murmured at the next round, and even Dex's eyebrows shot up at that. Tanner had said Dex could track about ninety percent of the cards dealt, but he couldn't track every single one.

"You're nuts, lady." The penguin shook his head. She had a queen and a seven — a good, high hand.

Karen, Tanner's worried voice entered her mind from across the room.

"Hit me," she insisted.

Dex shook his hand and flipped her another card, and a cry went up.

"A four! Twenty-one!" the Elvis fan cheered for her.

With her winnings inching steadily closer to the two million mark, Karen felt giddy with success. High, even, which should have turned on all her inner alarms.

Don't overdo it, Tanner cautioned her. *That has to be enough.*

She cracked her fingers and motioned for another hand. The showgirl grew nervous, shifting from foot to foot. Karen pushed the glasses higher on her nose and checked her watch.

Just one more round, her dragon whispered. *All we need is one more round.*

Dex's eyes darted around, and the play of his fingers over the cards gave his anxiety away.

Quick, her dragon urged. *Just one quick round.*

"I'm close to my break," Dex called to the showgirl. "Why don't you stay for a second and watch?"

Yes, Karen nearly added. *Stay right there. Don't move a feather.*

"Anything for you, honey," the showgirl said.

Anything for the twenty thousand I'm getting, the woman might as well have said, although the hitch in her voice said she was impatient to move on.

The showgirl's presence was a blessing and a curse. With the feathers keeping the camera covered, no one would be alerted to Karen's winning streak, but with the men all stealing glances at Amber, the game proceeded at a snail's pace.

Dex flicked cards over the table and tapped the table to get their attention. "Anyone?"

"Hit me," Freddie Mercury said.

Dealing the card to Freddie took an eternity, and Karen wiped her brow. She tapped the table, not quite satisfied with her hand.

"You want another card?" Red Lips asked incredulously. "When you have a nine and an eight?"

Yeah, it was a risk, but hell, she was on a roll now.

When Dex dealt her an ace, Karen sat back in relief. Eighteen. Another win.

"This is so exciting, I just don't want to leave," the showgirl announced from over her ear. In other words, *Hurry the hell up. I have to get out of here.*

A leathery hand pulled at her arm, and Karen turned to see Grandma Panda, looking like an empress in a high-necked silk dress and gold jewelry.

"Time we go. Time we go," the woman said in her quick, accented speech.

That had been arranged, too — along with the ten-thousand-dollar payment they had agreed on that afternoon. The panda would cash in Karen's chips so she could make a quicker exit.

Dex tapped his fingers on the table, urging her to call it a day.

All Karen had to do was sip her drink, pull out on the next round, then pick up her cash and meet Tanner outside. He had stashed his motorcycle nearby, and soon, they would be rolling over the highway with the wind in their hair. Once they hit Utah, they would transfer the others their cut of the winnings and move on with their own happily-ever-after.

Grandma Panda held out a silk bag with a Chinese dragon stitched on it. The chips Karen slid over the edge of the table made muffled little clanking sounds as they fell in.

She exhaled slowly. The hard part was over. She was nearly done.

The penguin shifter nodded his congratulations, and Dex wiped his glistening brow. They'd done it. There was a good two million in that bag.

One of the chips missed the bag and rolled under the table, though, and Freddie Mercury retrieved it for her.

"One more for the road?" He grinned.

She could feel temptation pulling on her like a puppet on a string. All the gambling she'd done that day was for Tanner's bear clan, not for herself. One more win with that ten-thousand-dollar chip could give her and Tanner a nice little nest egg.

"See you, Dex, honey." The showgirl sashayed off with her dance shoes clicking, her headdress fluttering.

It took all of Karen's self-resolve to take her last chip and stand up instead of betting one more time. But just as she stood, the space behind her filled again.

"Sir." Dex nodded to the newcomer. From the tilt of Dex's head, she knew the guy had to tower well over six feet. Closer to seven, maybe. A giraffe shifter, judging by the dry, savannah scent he carried with him.

That part hadn't been arranged, which only proved fate was on her side. The shifter stood right where Amber had, blocking the camera. Which meant she had time for one more bet, right?

Karen pushed her last chip into the betting box and said, "One more round."

Grandma Panda tut-tutted and shook her head in one of those *young-people-these-days* gestures and headed to the cashier with the mother lode of chips.

I'll be right there, her dragon called after the old woman. *Just one more round...*

A round that seemed to take an eternity.

"Just decide, already," Karen snapped when the penguin counted his chips for the twentieth time.

"I'm in with three thousand," he finally announced.

"I'm in with ten," she said, trying to move things along.

Everything seemed to proceed in ultra slow motion from then on. The cards Dex dealt fluttered across the table one by one. The penguin checked his cards four times. Lipstick lady doubled her bet. The woman at the end hummed louder, and even that stretched out to a low warble in Karen's mind.

She checked her cards. An ace and a two — thirteen.

"Hit me." She scratched the felt tabletop just to have something to do.

The penguin took another card, too, and ended with a strong nineteen. The dealer had a queen and a mystery card. Karen turned her third card over and slowly exhaled.

"A seven!" the Elvis fan called. "Wow. You really are on a roll."

When Dex turned his second card over and revealed a six, she released the breath she'd been holding and reached for her winnings. She'd done it! She'd really done it!

She tossed a thousand dollar chip at Dex as a tip and shifted her weight, ready to rise when the air pressure in the room cooled as if someone had flipped the air conditioning to high.

Dex's eyes widened on something behind her, and Karen's skin crawled.

"I'll just be going now," the penguin shifter mumbled in a jittery voice.

Karen wanted to do the same, but when she spun in her chair, every muscle in her body tensed.

Igor Schiller stood scowling at her with his arms crossed over his chest. Not a hair out of place, not a trace of color on his cheeks. Not a hint of warmth in his body. Elvira stood on his right wearing a sequined dress and an intense look of distaste. Four burly security guards flanked the pair.

Karen's heart sank, especially when she spotted Tanner behind them, his eyes wide with alarm. Obviously, Igor's change in plans was a surprise to him, too.

"Now, now," Schiller said in his death-chilled-over voice. "What do we have here?"

Chapter Sixteen

Holy. Crap.

Tanner clenched his hands into fists, trying to maintain a calm outer veneer. Which was nearly impossible with his bear bellowing to be freed.

Kill vampires! Grab mate! Get the hell out!

The beast was nearly as difficult to control as his temper. What the hell was Karen doing, lingering in the casino for so long?

She's winning the money we need for the land, his bear retorted. *Endangering herself for us.*

Which made it really hard to stay mad at her for being so reckless. But, hell. How was he going to get her out of there? Security guards were filing in from all sides, surrounding the table. Even Dex, who was always the picture of calm and cool, nervously shuffled and reshuffled the cards. The other guests at the table fled, which left Karen alone and as defiant and beautiful as ever, especially in that green silk dress that carried a shimmer of dragon magic in its cloth.

He sighed a little. Just his luck to fall for a headstrong dragon who didn't know when enough was enough.

His bear warmed a little at the thought.

"Such a pleasure to see you again, my dear," Schiller said in a sour tone.

"Can't say the feeling's mutual," Karen shot back.

Tanner kept his mouth closed and calculated the distance to the nearest exit. Far. Much too far, especially with seven or eight vampires closing in. He'd sensed Schiller coming a minute before the man had actually stepped through the casino doors, and though he'd hurried to intercept the vampire and buy Karen time, there had been too many guests in the way.

Kill! Attack! Maim! his bear screamed.

His fingernails bit into his palms as he barely held back. He couldn't bowl everyone out of the way because his only advantage was the element of surprise. Schiller and his men assumed he would back them up, so he had to play along until he spotted a chance to make his move.

Spot it soon, his bear growled.

"Nice hairdo," Elvira sneered. "And I love the glasses. Did you buy them at a dime store?"

The hair on the back of his neck prickled. Boy, would he love to wring Elvira's neck.

Karen patted her hair. "You like my hair? I told the woman who did it I wanted it just like yours." Elvira glowed a little until Karen finished. "You know, that fake, poofy look with enough hair spray to stop a speeding bullet or two."

"Bullets won't be necessary, my dear." Schiller showed his fangs.

Karen glared back. "You're right. I was thinking more along the lines of a stake through the heart. Holy water. Garlic. That kind of thing."

"It'll be your heart that's bleeding, honey," Elvira taunted, licking her lips.

Tanner saw Karen turn to her with another snappy response, but when her gaze caught on the gem shining from between Elvira's breasts, she stopped short.

The diamond, his bear whispered, sotto voice. *Elvira is wearing the Blood Diamond.*

Karen's eyes gleamed just like the diamond would when held up to the light. He could see her inner dragon rear up, just under the surface, as close to bursting out as his bear was.

Let me out! It's time to fight with claws and fangs instead of fists. To protect Karen. To get her out of here.

Tanner looked around, counting guards. He had to time his attack perfectly if he was to have any chance at success. Eight vampires, with another two coming up. Crap. A grizzly had a good chance of taking on two, maybe three vampires. But ten?

We don't have to win as long as Karen gets out alive, his bear grunted, ready to martyr himself.

If that's what it took, he would do it, but crap, wasn't there a better way?

Another vampire hurried up to the group. Shit — it was Antoine, the guard he'd hit over the head. "I told you she's a goddamned witch!"

"Half dragon," Schiller mulled over the syllables like a good brandy. "Half witch."

All the vampires licked their lips, making Tanner's skin crawl. They would suck him dry, too, when they discovered his double cross. He clenched his jaw. Well, he wouldn't go down without a fight, and as long as Karen escaped, he could die with some sense of satisfaction, right?

Karen's eyes were still pinned to the diamond, calculating, and his bear grew even more morose.

Well, even if she doesn't love us the way we love her, it will still be worth it, the beast sighed, seeing her so fixated on the diamond.

If one of the bear elders had been there, they would be sure to lean in and tap him on the shoulder. *Can't trust a witch, sonny. And as for dragons, well, all they care about are their jewels.*

Then Karen blinked — once, twice — and he stood perfectly still. Not breathing. Not moving. Not thinking. Just hoping with all his heart.

Her luminous eyes pulled away from the diamond and focused directly on him, and she smiled. *Smiled,* like she wasn't surrounded by a dozen angry vampires, all waiting to feast on her blood.

I love you, her eyes said.

I love you, he telegraphed back.

She nodded ever so slightly and looked around, calculating again. Then she rubbed her cheek with three fingers.

On three, she murmured into his mind.

Shit. What was she up to now?

Still, he nodded from his position behind the vampires. If there had ever been a time for spontaneity, this had to be it. What exactly Karen planned to do on three, he wasn't sure. Frankly, he would bet she didn't know yet either. But he was all in.

"The perfect combination for a midnight feast," Schiller continued, confirming his fears that there would be no luxury lockup for Karen this time.

Terrible images of Karen pinned to the floor, struggling against Schiller's fangs engulfed Tanner, and his blood boiled. And while the images sickened him, he hung on to them, letting them fuel his bear's rage.

One, Karen's look said.

He rolled to the balls of his feet, ready to take out the two closest vampires from behind.

"Far from perfect. . . " Elvira sniffed.

"Not as far as you," Karen shot back in the same breath she signaled, *Two.*

". . . but I suppose she'll do," Elvira continued, ignoring the insult.

Karen rolled her eyes up at the ceiling, worked her jaw left and right, and then met his gaze.

Ready for three?

Tanner let his fingernails extend into bear claws and shifted his weight. Hell yes, was he ready.

Karen threw her head back, coughed, and sparks popped out of her mouth.

Elvira cackled. "You call that a fire? Of course, if you're only half dragon—"

Karen snapped her fingers. "And half witch." She coughed again, and *whoosh!* The sparks ignited into a huge, licking flame aimed straight at the ceiling.

Elvira screamed. The vampires stepped back, raising their hands against the blazing light.

Three! Karen shouted in his mind.

Tanner bared his teeth and let his claws rip.

Whoosh! Karen shot another volley of flames in a huge, fiery arc.

Thump! The first vampire fell to the floor, his throat ripped out by Tanner's claws. A second dropped beside him, dead before he hit the red carpet.

Tanner bellowed and charged the next vampire as the area exploded into shouts and cries.

"Fight! Fight!"

"Fire! Fire!"

The words set off a stampede for the exits as alarms whooped and the sprinkler system kicked in.

"My hair!" Elvira wailed, trying to cover herself with her blood-red scarf.

Tanner caught a brief glimpse of Dex, looking his way.

Need help? the panther's expression asked.

Tanner sliced a hand through the air, flashing a quick stop sign. *Not your fight, bro.*

Dex was a hell of a fighter to have on his side, but if the panther could maintain his undercover role, they would have an ace up their sleeve if things went really wrong.

As they were fairly sure to do, knowing Karen's hastily formed plans. Make that his hastily formed plans, too.

Dex ducked out of sight behind the upturned table.

"You!" Schiller hissed, stepping toward Karen. Water from the sprinklers plastered his hair to his scalp and streaked his tailored suit.

Tanner body-checked two guards out of the way, trying to reach Schiller in time.

"You," Karen said calmly, sending her next flame straight at the vampire.

Igor ducked and rolled for cover, and — *Whoa!* — Tanner dodged the farthest lick of fire.

Sorry! Karen yelped.

Hell, your fire is resistant to water. Handy trick. He nodded her way.

He'd never seen Karen look prouder than just then. Not that he had much time to admire her. He spun on his heel and swung his claws left just as Antoine aimed a punch at his kidneys. Antoine missed, but Tanner didn't, and four parallel lines of sickly blue-red blood showed on the vampire's cheek. Tanner roared and sliced again, this time garroting the vampire's neck. A good thing the entire casino was in pandemonium — none of the screams seemed to be a response to that particular emergency. The fire had spread to the banners hung from the ceiling, and guests stumbled frantically through the thick veil of water raining from the sprinklers.

"Watch out!" Karen yelled.

Two fingers of yellow flame blazed by his ear as he stumbled from a blow from another attacker. He rolled, leaped to his knees, and batted at the vampire with a massive claw. That much of the bear, he let out. The rest he kept leashed, if barely. It would be a lot easier to make a getaway in human form.

"No!" Karen yelped, and his head whipped around. A vampire had snuck up behind her and was dragging her away while Schiller stalked closer.

"I've had quite enough of you, my dear girl," the vampire muttered as his guards closed ranks around Karen.

Never had a pale vampire face gone so red with anger, and never had Schiller sounded as malicious as then. But Tanner had never felt quite so big or angry either, and when he charged, bodies flew. Vampires grunted. Blood splashed. Sharp nails scraped his skin, and inhumanly strong punches pounded his body while he battled to his mate's side.

The chandelier shook when Tanner roared in his bear voice. He hurled another vampire against the wall, shattering a mirror.

"Run for it!" Karen called.

As if he would ever leave her. As if he would turn his back on the woman he loved.

The flames Karen cast grew weaker, either from the sprinklers or a counter-spell cast by the casino's witches. Schiller wheeled from Karen to him, and his dark eyes narrowed in rage.

"You."

If Tanner had been Karen, he would have had a smart ass retort for the vampire. But he was just a bear, and bears spoke in a different way.

With a swipe of his massive claw, he sent Schiller flying backward across the blackjack table, packing in the rage and power of a dozen grizzlies.

"Tanner," Karen said, now that they were finally face-to-face.

"Karen," he managed.

"Let's get out of here, shall we?"

He nodded. "Yes. Let's." He stared down the last vampires standing in his way.

"Um..." one of them mumbled, looking at another.

"Uh..." a second stammered.

Tanner stalked forward, and they both shuffled back.

Good, his bear growled.

"Just a second." Karen pulled her hand out of his.

He nearly tossed her over his shoulder and bulldozed his way to the door. No way were they stopping now. But Elvira was cowering behind an overturned table, and Karen snatched the diamond off her neck.

"I'll be taking this," she said, then hurried to his side.

Tanner pulled her to the door, ignoring Elvira's screeches.

"Ouch! Do you have to crush my hand?" Karen complained as he hustled her along.

"Yep." No way was he risking his mate doing anything impulsive again.

"Just...just..." Karen protested as they ran for the glass doors and onto the sidewalk, where the fresh night air gave him the first taste of freedom he'd had in far too long. "Wait!"

He didn't wait, but he did let her steer him to where Grandma Panda waited.

"Thank you!" Karen cried, grabbing at the woman's bag. It swung and hit his leg with a dull thump, not a sharp clink, which meant the panda had succeeded in trading the chips for cash before all hell had broken loose.

"You're welcome!" The elderly panda patted a purse thick with her cut of the deal.

"That way." He pointed Karen through the crowd milling outside. The vampires would be after him in no time, because he had (a) Karen, whose blood they coveted, (b) two million dollars of their money, and (c) the diamond. He shook his head as he ran, wondering how he'd ever gotten that deep into trouble.

Would you want it any other way? His bear grinned.

No, he supposed he didn't. But he sure would celebrate when they crossed the state border into Idaho. Shit, he would be looking over his shoulder for most of the eight hundred miles home.

Nah. We taught these vampires a lesson. They'll stay the hell away, his bear said.

God, he hoped so.

"Hop on." He threw a leg over the motorcycle he'd left parked nearby.

Karen shoved the money bag into the leather pannier, then wiggled onto the seat behind him. When she pressed her body close, he smiled for the first time in what seemed like days. Her words made his grin even wider.

"Take me home, bear. Take me home."

Chapter Seventeen

Karen leaned forward to kiss Tanner's cheek. When he gunned the engine, scattering the crowd, she grabbed his waist. For now, that peck on the cheek would have to do. But later — man, would she have a lot more kisses ready to make everything up to him. A lot of apologizing, too, because she really had pushed her luck that time.

More like, you stretched your luck into the thinnest possible thread and sprinted across a chasm like a tightwire act, a stern voice in the back of her mind said as the motorcycle hit Las Vegas Boulevard and gathered speed.

She nearly shot back a comment but buried her face in the fabric covering Tanner's broad back instead.

Okay, okay, maybe I did.

Maybe?

Definitely.

What happened to turning over a new leaf?

She gulped and counted to ten, then counted again, because she'd never meant to risk that much. She'd never meant to risk Tanner's money or his life.

She kept her face hidden there for a good long time, lecturing herself.

Will never defy vampires again. No matter what.

Will keep my mouth shut when possible. Will really, really try.

Will tell this bear what he means to me, every day for the rest of my life.

"Hey," Tanner called over his shoulder. "You okay?"

The motorcycle rolled over the smooth surface of Highway 15, heading north — right for the Great Bear's tail, it seemed, when she looked over Tanner's shoulder. The sky was full of stars, the night cool and crisp and clear. She tucked her hands into the pockets of his jacket and reveled in the crisp wind blowing through her hair. She wondered what to say, where to start.

"Thanks." She vowed to try out another thousand variations of that word, because it didn't quite capture what she meant. "I'm good," she added, though it didn't even begin to say what she wanted to express.

Tanner was better at two-word speeches than she was, because his tone captured everything just right. "Thank you," he murmured over his shoulder. The words caressed her ear before the wind whipped them away.

"I'm sorry," she blurted a second later.

"About what?"

"About everything." She'd screwed up again. She'd gambled with their lives.

"I'm not." Tanner caressed her hand.

She pressed her cheek against his back and rubbed up and down. What had she done to deserve the world's best bear?

"Another hundred miles and—" The motorcycle swerved.

She popped her head up. "What?"

"Shit." Tanner looked at the sideview mirror.

"What?" she cried, then gulped. "Oh, God."

The lights of several big, black SUVs lit the highway behind them, closing fast.

"Schiller?" She hoped Tanner would name someone — any-one! — else.

"Schiller," he replied in a flat tone.

"Shit." She stared at the speedometer, then looked over her shoulder. The vampires were definitely gaining. Now, what?

Tanner revved the motorcycle higher, but the off-road tires kept the bike from building much speed.

"Crap," he muttered when it was clear they couldn't out-race the vampires.

She looked back, feeling the heat rise in her face. She'd had enough of Igor fucking Schiller and his bloodsucking gang.

"Hang on," Tanner said in that even, calm tone he used whenever things spiraled out of control.

The engine roared as he bounced the bike off the highway and into the open scrub. The wheels of the SUVs squealed when they followed suit, kicking up a dust cloud that hung in the pale moonlight.

"Crap." She clutched Tanner as they bounced over a lunar landscape of rocks and low scrubs.

"We got this," Tanner murmured, though she knew it was for show. Even off-road, how were they going to outrun four SUVs?

A powerful searchlight hit them, and a thunderous crack split the night.

"Whoa!" She ducked and hung on when Tanner swerved, nearly ditching her. When he roared on, another two cracks broke out above the noise of straining engines and scattered rocks. "They're shooting at us now?"

He nodded. "Silver bullets, I'd bet."

"What?" She wanted to stomp the ground and scream. To shake her hand and point an accusing finger. To yell to the world that it wasn't fair. How dare those vampires utilize one of the few weapons that could kill a creature as formidable as her bear?

Her bear, damn it!

How dare they? her dragon demanded, raging inside her.

And just like that, her vision went red.

She had put Tanner in danger.

She had drawn the wrath of the vampires again and again, and they'd come after her again and again.

Well, she'd had it. Absolutely, positively had it. She'd been degraded. Insulted. Locked up. Ridiculed. And now it was time to take her revenge. To prove herself, once and for all.

Revenge! her dragon growled.

Rage overwhelmed every thought and emotion until nothing mattered but beating the vampires — and proving herself.

Believe. . . Her grandfather's voice echoed in her ears. *You have to believe.*

117

And just like that, she knew what to do, and she knew she could do it. She believed.

"Follow that trail." She pointed over Tanner's shoulder at a two-track dirt road. "Keep us as steady as you can."

"What are you doing?" He grabbed for her arm.

She drew her knees up and held his shoulders with both hands. "I have an idea."

"Not again," he groaned.

"A good one," she insisted. There was no time for doubt, for second guesses.

"Yeah, well—"

Before he could finish his sentence, she drew a foot up, then a knee, and then—

"Are you nuts?" he yelled.

"Don't slow down!" she ordered, getting to her feet.

She'd tried a few tricks on horseback in her time, but holy crap, standing on the seat of a motorcycle while it hammered down a dirt track was different. Very different.

Believe, her dragon chanted. *Clear your mind and believe.*

She crouched behind Tanner, hanging on to his shoulders.

"Karen!" he protested.

"Just keep it straight. Straight and fast."

Yes, she was nuts. Yes, she was impulsive. But her dragon was roaring inside her in a way it never had before.

I can do this. Trust me. Let me try.

Trying won't cut it, she snapped back.

I can do it. Watch. Trust, her dragon roared.

The only reason she didn't snort and say, *Forget it* was the Blood Diamond. She'd sensed the energy pulsing off it the first time she'd seen the jewel, and holding it was like holding a hot ember. She could feel the power in it throb.

That diamond holds the power of our ancestors, her grandfather had told her. *And the dragon who holds it can harness that power. Make it his own.*

His own or her own? she'd joked at the time. They'd laughed, but she sure wasn't laughing now.

Trust me. I can do this, her dragon said.

She closed her eyes and felt the wind whip her hair. Imagined what it would feel like if she were flying in dragon form. Flying, not gliding. Real flying. If her grandfather's power had buoyed her that one time she'd really flown, the power of the Blood Diamond would truly make her soar.

I can do it.

Karen clutched Tanner's shirt.

We can do it. Her dragon nodded.

Karen took a deep breath and jumped into the air.

"Karen!" Tanner shouted, but his voice was faint. The noise of the engine was faint, too, as was everything but the voice in her mind.

I can do it. Watch me fly.

She stretched tall, reaching for the stars, and spread her arms wide. And while half of her expected to crash and be crushed under the oncoming tires of the SUVs, the other half believed. Really believed in the power of the Blood Diamond, if not herself.

Fly. I can fly. I will fly.

And holy crap, she did. An updraft caught her under the wings — partway through her jump, she'd shifted to dragon form in the blink of an eye — and sent her soaring. Up, up, up, as high as the hills slumbering in the distance.

Now bank around, her dragon murmured, concentrating hard.

She bent her right wing the teensiest, tiniest bit and curved in a wide, cautious loop. She bent it a little more to tighten the turn then flicked that wing straight and bent the left one, banking the other way. She turned one way then the other, getting the hang of it. Soon, she was shrieking with delight.

I'm flying! Really flying!

She squeezed her eyelids until they were mere slits, a barrier to the whipping effect of the wind, and flapped her ears a few times, just to relish the flow of the air over them. It was even better than she imagined. More exhilarating. Intoxicating, even.

A gunshot cracked below her, and she snapped back to her senses. Shit — she had vampires to vanquish. The world's

119

most persistent bear to kiss. No time to simply enjoy flying.
Not at a time like this.

Chapter Eighteen

Headlights swept the desert below — three pairs of headlights from the SUVs, a blindingly bright spotlight aimed from the roof of a fourth, and the dim, single lamp of the motorcycle that wound a crooked path through the scrub.

Save bear! Kill vampires!

Karen folded her wings and dove, howling with a mixture of rage and glee. Exactly the way she might dive into water, except it was thin air. The best part was, she dove with confidence, because the Blood Diamond was empowering her, and it would never let her down.

The wind whistled off her wingtips while her mind played a soundtrack of bomber planes zooming in on their target. The closer the SUVs drew, the angrier she became, and the more her dragon took over her mind. What right did they have to come between her and her mate? How dare they?

She pulled back her lips, bared her teeth, and inhaled deeply.

Sayonara, assholes, her dragon cried.

She coughed up a spark, exhaled, and — *whoosh!* A huge, licking flame engulfed the vehicle closest to Tanner. She blew until the flames split over both sides of the roof and rushed over the windows.

The vehicle jerked in a tight right turn. So tight, the SUV tipped over and lay on its side, where she gave it another blast for good measure before sweeping upward again. The doors flew open and vampires clambered out.

If only she could spit pure fire like the dragons of generations past! Her magick-enhanced fire wasn't dense enough to be lethal to vampires, so she couldn't kill them, but seeing them run like panicked chickens was satisfying, too.

She gained altitude with a few flaps of her wings and cackled with a crazy kind of joy. She could dive! Turn! Climb high in the sky! She could really fly!

A whisper on the wind carried a hint of her grandfather's voice. *Of course, you can.*

Tanner's voice was the second to sound in her mind. *Of course, you can.*

She flapped her wings, rushing after the next two vehicles driving alongside each other in pursuit of the motorcycle.

Perfect, her dragon purred.

She blasted them from behind, spraying a jet of fire from side to side to reach both vehicles, keeping it up even after one banged into the other and both careened into a rocky outcrop. A moment later, vampires spilled from the vehicles, rushing away, and she bombed them with flames. The fire made a rushing, rocket sound when she propelled it. Together with the frantic movements of the vampires, it made her imagine an apocalypse. Fire and brimstone! Pandemonium! The best part was that *she* was the one making it happen — on purpose, not by some freaky accident. And even though she'd always had it drilled into her that self-respecting dragons never used their powers for destruction, these were vampires, and they had it coming, right?

Right, she decided, looking around.

Three vehicles down, one to go — the SUV with the bright spotlight, which was still in hot pursuit of Tanner. Without her on the back of the bike, he seemed to be holding his own, but then a rifle shot split the night, and she remembered the danger her mate was in.

Not for long, her dragon muttered, extending its neck.

She curled her wings, rolled right, and then leveled out and sped ahead. Schiller was in that SUV — she could sense it — so she had to make this pass count.

Within seconds, she was half a mile ahead of Tanner, scoping out the landscape. There — an upslope that ended in a sheer cliff. She glanced back and slowed, hoping Tanner would follow her lead.

Another crazy escape plan? His voice was faint in her mind.

She grinned. *Not so crazy. Just watch the cliff.*

She could sense him snort. *"Just" and "cliff" don't really go together, you know.*

There's a trail that turns off right here — she made a sharp left to indicate the spot — *and then you can follow the edge.*

The edge? Why don't I like the sound of that?

She would have loved to keep up the banter, but she had a truck full of vampires to outsmart. And this time, damn it, she would do it.

Curving her wings, she twisted and raced straight for Tanner and the SUV behind him. And damn, did the distance shrink quickly now that she was low to the ground and rushing at them head on.

Karen! Holy— Tanner ducked.

At the last possible second, she gave her tail a little flick and cleared him by an inch.

—shit! he finished, speeding toward the cliff.

She barreled straight at the SUV and opened her jaws wide. The vampire hanging out the side window with a rifle at his shoulder jerked inside just as she slammed the vehicle with another massive blast of fire. The SUV shuddered from the force of it but rushed on, even with flames washing over the windshield and along both sides. Karen barely pulled up in time to clear it.

Whoa! The antenna scratched her belly as she scraped over the roof.

As the vehicle sped on, the flames extinguished. So, shit — maybe she wasn't the only witch casting spells in the desert just then. She turned and raced after the SUV, which was gaining on Tanner fast. Really fast.

Hurry! she urged him. *Faster!*

I got this, he murmured into her mind as he glanced over his shoulder.

The SUV was so close, she couldn't spit fire at it without hitting Tanner, so she curved away and looped around to come at it from the side.

From her height, she could see both vehicles rapidly approaching the cliff — a blind cliff hidden by a tiny dip and rise.

Turn! she screamed into Tanner's mind. *Turn!*

He didn't waver. Not an inch.

Now! Turn now! she yelled.

A second longer and Tanner would miss the tight turn to the hiker's trail that paralleled the edge of the cliff. He would be airborne. He would crash and die.

Turn, damn it! Turn!

She watched in horror, helpless to intervene as both vehicles raced closer to the drop-off. Closer and closer—

Tanner threw the bike into a bruising ninety-degree turn, jamming his left foot against the ground to prevent it from skidding over the ledge. And the SUV—

Brakes screeched. Dust flew. The horn blew, and the whole vehicle skipped and shuddered toward the edge of the cliff.

From the corner of her eye, Karen saw Tanner level out, drive a hundred feet, then stop to look back.

The wheels of the SUV plowed deep furrows into the ground as its headlights stabbed over the lip of the cliff. Finally, it came to rest with its front tires an inch from the cliff. Her heart sank. She could practically hear Schiller's triumphant cackle when he stepped out of the car.

But then the lip of the cliff groaned and gave way, and the front tires tipped over the edge. Five thousand pounds of steel teetered. One of the doors popped open, and a terrified vampire clung to it, looking for a way out.

Rage flooded Karen's mind again, and she went from an easy hover to all-out dive, blasting a long spear of flames. She imagined fire forming a battering ram, giving the SUV just enough of a bump to send it over the edge.

Metal groaned, flames hissed, and a vampire screamed, leaping from the SUV a split second before it tipped slowly forward. Then it was airborne, flipping end over end until — *Boom!* It came to a fiery crash and exploded below.

Karen flinched at the explosion, then admired the sight — for all of five seconds before turning back for Schiller. The vampire stood at the edge of the cliff, smeared with ash and dust. His eyes widened when he saw her coming, and he dove for cover just before her next blast hit.

For the next few minutes, Karen played the best game of cat and mouse ever, chasing the vampire from one rocky outcrop to the next with little bursts of fire. She might not be able to kill Schiller, but hell, she could humiliate him a bit.

Um, Karen? a deep voice tapped at the edge of her mind.

She popped her head up in mid flight. *Yeah?*

You done yet?

She shot a parting ball of fire at Schiller, then doubled back to the cliff's edge where a lone figure stood out before a startlingly clear, starry sky. She circled once, twice, not quite ready to stop flying — Who knew if she would ever manage to get aloft again? — but plenty ready to reunite with her mate. When she folded her wings and landed, little puffs of dust rose from the ground.

Her eyes locked on Tanner's, and they stood in silence, listening to the distant crackle of fire, the chirp of cicadas, the murmur of the night breeze over desert chaparral. Tanner had turned off the engine, so the only light was that of the stars above, the fire below, and the glow of Vegas on the horizon.

"We did it," she whispered at long last.

Tanner nodded, not taking his eyes off her. "You did it."

She raked her foot through the sand, slowly transforming to human form, and what started as a claw finished the motion as a bare foot.

Tanner's eyes flicked over her bare chest and legs, and a tiny smile formed in the corner of his mouth.

"You're naked."

She laughed. "Can't seem to help it around you."

He grinned then shook his head incredulously, looking around the sky as if replaying her flight. "That was amazing."

She tried an *aw-shucks* shrug, but her body refused to play along, standing tall and proud — until two hundred pounds of bear shifter stepped over and wrapped her in a massive hug.

"You did it." He ran his hands over her hair, her shoulders, and her back, checking for broken bones.

A balloon of pride filled in her chest, because even if it had been the diamond fueling her, she could claim some of the credit, right? But a dragon shouldn't get too full of herself, as her grandfather had warned so many times, so she pulled away to explain.

"I could only fly because of the diamond. But still, it was pretty cool."

Tanner tilted his head. "What do you mean, because of the diamond?"

"The diamond holds the power of the ancient dragons, and it gives—"

He cut her off. "I remember that. But what does that have to do with you flying?"

She laughed. The poor guy had obviously had too long a day. He couldn't think straight any more.

"I've never managed anything more than gliding before. The diamond gave me the power to fly."

He squinted at her. "The diamond gave you the power from all the way down here?"

"No, I had it with me." Silly bear.

"No, I had it with me." Tanner patted the side of his jacket.

"I had it with me. Right here." She patted her chest, where the necklace would be—

—and immediately panicked, because the diamond wasn't there. God, had she lost it? Had it been ripped off when she shifted to dragon form?

Oh, God. Oh, God. Oh, God. Her dragon started fretting. She'd screwed everything up — again.

"No," Tanner said slowly, pulling something out of his pocket. "I have it with me."

He uncurled his fingers and there it was — the Blood Diamond, glinting with the light of a thousand stars.

Karen opened her mouth. Moved her lips. Tried to work her tongue, but it just flopped limply. In her mind, she replayed their escape from the casino. Hadn't she looped the necklace over her head on the way out of the Scarlet Palace?

Wait — she'd been about to, but then Grandma Panda had come along, so she'd kept the jewel in her hand.

Hop on. She remembered Tanner motioning her onto the motorcycle.

She played the memory forward in her mind slowly. When Tanner gunned the engine, she'd slipped her hands inside his jacket pockets for a better grip around his waist, leaving the diamond there.

Tanner grabbed her hand just as she keeled over in surprise.

"Whoa, there." He grinned and wrapped her hand over the diamond. "See?"

See? Sure. She could feel it, too — not just the hard edges digging into her palm but the pulsing energy that went right from the stone to her soul. She could sense it, buoying her up.

But believe it? She wasn't quite there yet. If Tanner had had the diamond all along, that meant...

"Oh my God," she whispered. "I did it. I flew on my own."

He shrugged. "Of course, you did."

There was no hint of surprise or wonder in his voice at all, only faith. Unshakable, unwavering faith, as if he'd known it all along.

She stared.

A dragon's powers are kindled by love, and if you truly believe... Maybe her grandfather hadn't been kidding her, after all.

Tanner crooked an eyebrow at her. "Speechless? That's a change."

She smacked him on the shoulder, though he didn't budge. He just laughed and pulled a spare shirt out of his saddlebag. "Here. Ready to go?"

"Boy, am I." She pulled the shirt on, followed by his leather jacket. They both smelled like Tanner, all fresh and woodsy. Like home. She zipped the jacket high and inhaled, then pulled on a pair of pants. "Definitely ready to go."

He kicked the motorcycle engine on and waited for her to climb on the back before starting down the trail.

"Where to?" she called over his shoulder.

"Home." He pointed forward, more toward the stars than to any particular place.

"And where exactly would that be?" It was more a tease than a question, because any place he took her would be fine with her.

"I know just the place for a bear and a dragon-witch to settle down."

"Oh, yeah?"

"Yeah. A little cabin high in the Bitterroot Mountains. Plenty of mountain streams for you to prospect in, and just enough lumbering to keep me busy."

"Not too busy, I hope." She slid her hands lower along his bulky frame.

He laughed. "I promise I'll find some spare time."

She could already picture hitting the sheets of a king-size bed covered with a patchwork quilt stitched with a pattern of pines. Going to sleep in his arms and waking up in them, too — not for a single day or night, but an entire lifetime.

"We don't want life to get boring," she added, lest he think she was going soft.

Tanner laughed outright. "Is that a promise or a threat?"

She snuggled closer and shut her eyes, listening to the engine hum.

"It's a promise, my love. A promise."

Sneak Peek: Gambling on Her Panther

Panther shifter Dex Davitt has just earned himself a cool million dollars. The problem? Leaving Las Vegas with his loot — alive. Why? Well, that's complicated. *Falling desperately in love* kind of complicated. *Vengeful, bloodsucking vampires* complicated. *Carefully laid plans falling apart* kind of complicated. Is it all just a run of bad luck, or is it destiny?

Ex-stuntwoman Dakota Morgenstern is ready to be an ex-Las Vegas business owner too. And she's more than ready to trade Sin City for a quieter, simpler life on a ranch. There's just one catch — a sinfully charming card dealer who may have inadvertently gambled with both of their lives.

Books by Anna Lowe

Shifters in Vegas

Paranormal romance with a zany twist

Gambling on Trouble

Gambling on Her Dragon

Gambling on Her Bear

Gambling on Her Panther

Aloha Shifters - Jewels of the Heart

Lure of the Dragon (Book 1)

Lure of the Wolf (Book 2)

Lure of the Bear (Book 3)

Lure of the Tiger (Book 4)

Love of the Dragon (Book 5)

Lure of the Fox (Book 6)

Aloha Shifters - Pearls of Desire

Rebel Dragon (Book 1)

Rebel Bear (Book 2)

Rebel Lion (Book 3)

Rebel Wolf (Book 4)

Rebel Heart (A prequel to Book 5)

Rebel Alpha (Book 5)

Fire Maidens - Billionaires & Bodyguards

Fire Maidens: Paris (Book 1)

Fire Maidens: London (Book 2)

Fire Maidens: Rome (Book 3)

Fire Maidens: Portugal (Book 4)

Fire Maidens: Ireland (Book 5)

Fire Maidens: Scotland (Book 6)

Fire Maidens: Venice (Book 7)

Fire Maidens: Greece (Book 8)

Fire Maidens: Switzerland (Book 9)

The Wolves of Twin Moon Ranch

Desert Hunt (the Prequel)

Desert Moon (Book 1)

Desert Blood (Book 2)

Desert Fate (Book 3)

Desert Heart (Book 4)

Desert Rose (Book 5)

Desert Roots (Book 6)

Desert Yule (a short story)

Desert Wolf: Complete Collection (Four short stories)

Sasquatch Surprise (a Twin Moon spin-off story)

Blue Moon Saloon

Perfection (a short story prequel)

Damnation (Book 1)

Temptation (Book 2)

Redemption (Book 3)

Salvation (Book 4)

Deception (Book 5)

Celebration (a holiday treat)

Serendipity Adventure Romance

Off the Charts

Uncharted

Entangled

Windswept

Adrift

Travel Romance

Veiled Fantasies

Island Fantasies

www.annalowebooks.com

About the Author

USA Today and Amazon bestselling author Anna Lowe loves putting the "hero" back into heroine and letting location ignite a passionate romance. She likes a heroine who is independent, intelligent, and imperfect – a woman who is doing just fine on her own. But give the heroine a good man – not to mention a chance to overcome her own inhibitions – and she'll never turn down the chance for adventure, nor shy away from danger.

Anna loves dogs, sports, and travel – and letting those inspire her fiction. On any given weekend, you might find her hiking in the mountains or hunched over her laptop, working on her latest story. Either way, the day will end with a chunk of dark chocolate and a good read.

Visit AnnaLoweBooks.com

Printed in Great Britain
by Amazon